Sweet OBLIVION

PART 1 OF THE OBLIVION SERIES

BY ALEXA PADGETT

ISBN-978-1-945090-32-5

Editor: Jessica Royer Ocken
Proofreading by: Charity Chimni
Cover by: Chris Philpot

For Charity.

I'm so thankful to call you a friend.

Tonic
Aya

I fell in love in less than one second. I looked it up, years later, to see if that really could have happened. The answer is yes. In five-tenths of a second, dopamine and oxytocin swelled and flowed from my brain, and I felt love pour through all my cells.

It was a rush I wanted to hit over and over again.

But I didn't get that chance.

I was five years old. On vacation. And as he walked away, I was sure I'd never again see the blond boy I'd given both my heart and the most perfect seashell.

Chapter 1
Aya

I splayed out in the silky, hot, white sand on the beach near my parents. The tip of my tongue slipped between my teeth as I worked the toothpick into the damp granules to create a chain link for my sand castle like I'd seen on the real castles in Paris. Mummy and Father spoke in quiet voices, but I could hear the strain, the tears, in my mummy's tone. My father's voice rose, surly, the words hurtful.

"Those were dreams of youth, Sofia. We're parents, and we need to focus on our future."

I didn't like the way he spoke to my mummy.

I rose from my spot under the shade of the large umbrella and shuffled closer to the water—then closer again so the cool seafoam slithered around my foot, causing me to giggle. I wiggled my toes, sinking my feet deeper into the powdery sand.

I stepped deeper into the waves, enjoying how the water cooled my hot legs. With a gasp of delight, I bent down and picked up a shell. I ran my other palm over the conch. The pink interior was smooth as satin. I clasped the shell in my fist and bent at the waist, searching for another.

"You shouldn't be out there by yourself."

I turned my head, squinting at the shape of a boy. He was bigger than me—most people were. Before I could answer, a wave causing him to slam his mouth shut and blush, tossing a glance at Gemma Cordova, the roadie's fifteen-year-old daughter. That hadn't happened to Lev in a while—not since he was about my age. Now, at fourteen, he seemed so much older. Well, until he wanted to impress this girl.

Gemma remained transfixed by the new song, unaware of Lev's self-consciousness. Pride swelled so hard that it pressed against my ribs, a happy bubble I never wanted to pop.

When Dad arrived in the green room after the show, he came right over and hugged me. "You see that reaction? Nash, my boy, we're on to something huge." His eyes twinkled.

I wrinkled my nose at the sweet cloy of perfume and the smear of red across his lip and cheek. Before I could ask him about it, a group of women tumbled into the room, beelining toward my father, all screaming *Braaaad.* He chuckled as he threw open his arms, stepping forward.

He winked at me and Lev. "The benefits of fame."

"He's such a douche," Lev muttered as he turned away.

Somewhere in the past year, Lev's devotion to our father had melted into deep-seated disdain.

"Why?" I asked.

Lev sucked on his drink—I was pretty sure he'd spiked his Coke with one of the bottles of liquor sitting on the overladen buffet tables, but I didn't ask. We were touring with a rock band, and as Lev said, *when in Rome…*

"He got a blow job backstage from one chick, and now he's going to bang at least one more."

My stomach curdled as I watched Dad wrap his arm around a curvaceous blonde with big, teased hair.

"Her shirt barely covers the underside of her tits," Lev muttered, grimacing. "And her shorts don't cover her ass cheeks. Classy."

"But…Mom…"

Lev snorted. "Is shooting that perfume ad in Paris." He turned to me, dark eyes serious. "And we're not going to tell her what goes on here. Because she'd cry more."

Lev's hands fisted so hard he broke his plastic cup and his drink rained down on his new Air Jordan sneakers and jeans.

"But…"

Lev growled as Dad bent to kiss the woman. I shuddered at the aggressive way he stuck his tongue in her mouth.

"Dad's a cheat, Nash," Lev said, voice flat. "I caught him, and he laughed." Lev's pale skin mottled. "This is why I'm glad Mom isn't here. She's had so much success while Dad's struggled."

My jaw dropped. "He has?"

"Yeah, man. Your songs—they're killer. Way better than Quantum's last two albums. From what I heard, this one'll go gold, maybe platinum." He pulled me in close and noogied my head. "Because of you."

"But…"

Lev glanced back at Dad and the woman, a ripple of displeasure shooting through his arms as he released me. "Look, maybe now that they're both successful it'll be better." His eyes pleaded with me. "Right?"

My stomach twisted. "I…" Something cracked in Lev's eyes,

and I grabbed his hand like I used to, when I was really little. He let me. "You're right, Lev. Now that they're both successful, everything's going to be better."

"We're going back to the hotel," he said with one last glare at our dad. "Don't look," he muttered, tugging me toward the door and our security detail.

I trailed behind him, the high from the night buried under the weight of the news that my father was a cheater—and that my songs might be the only thing that could keep my family together.

Chapter 3
TWO YEARS LATER
Nash

Three months in, I'd deemed ninth grade even more obnoxious than middle school, which had been my own personal hell. Clothes, expensive car rides, and even personalized, nonjudgmental learning environments failed to create decent humans here at Austin's elite Holyoke School. This was never more apparent than when my mom was in the news *again* for yet another substance-induced meltdown.

But mostly, this year caused an unbearable ache because once again, Lev wasn't here to share it with me. He wasn't here to share anything with me anymore. He was dead. And it *sucked* that I had to do this alone.

As much as I wanted to hunch under my backpack straps, I stood straight and tall, my brand-new Chuck Taylors thumping against the stained concrete hallway. My shoulders tensed as Lord Prescott, the leading private-school douche-monkey, rounded the corner. Like me, he wore black athletic pants and a brightly colored T-shirt. Mine had the logo of my father's band, Quantum, and Lord's said, *I can't be responsible for my face when you talk.*

His hair was spiked up in front because he couldn't manage the pouf most boys seemed to prefer, but he had added the requisite black beanie that sagged down his thick neck. Lord was a couple of inches shorter than me now. Over the long, hard, grief-filled summer, I'd started to shoot up and fill out. But Lord's viciousness ran at least as deep as his confidence, and he'd picked me out last year, right after Lev's death.

"How's it going, Nashville?" Lord asked with a smirk. Animosity slithered through his dark eyes.

I noted three additional boys, all muscular and with similar vapid expressions, behind him, and my quick scan of the hall showed it was free of teachers. Lord always waited for the teachers to disappear before he baited and hurt people.

I didn't even bother to roll my eyes and the lameness of his joke about my name, but I did hear the first, faint stirrings of a song. I strained, desperate for the melody…but it faded.

Damn Lord for getting my hopes up. I hadn't been able to write music since I'd watched my dad screw around with the groupies—first on that last tour and then at every one of the local shows I'd attended since. I'd already been angry with him, and then Lev's death had decimated me, and now I wasn't sure if I'd ever crawl out of this hole.

My father's frustrated comments this morning trickled through my mind. *"It's time to buckle down and get serious, Nash. I need to finish this album, which means I need more songs."* He hadn't followed that up with his usual comforting shoulder squeeze. In fact, he'd strode out of the house without so much as telling me to have a good day.

"Leave me alone, Lord. I'm not in the mood."

"Aw… Not feeling so hot these days, Nashville?" Lord taunted.

My dad had tons of worries and photo ops on his mind.

Quantum needed a new album in order to start their world tour. The single we'd cowritten before everything went to shit had burned its way up the charts, causing fans to clamor for more, but that tour I'd gone on with Lev was long gone—not unlike my ability to compose a tune.

I refocused on Lord, the perfect outlet for my anger, my worry over my father's frustration—everything.

"Considering my parents like me enough to stay in the same city, I'm good," I told him.

Lord snarled, his buggy eyes narrowing to a squint as his hands fisted. I held my ground, waiting, though I rolled up on the balls of my feet and tensed, readying for a blow.

"Your mom isn't here—" Lord began.

Hugh Peckham materialized next to me as I cut him off. Lord wasn't going to say *anything* about my mother. "What do your parents do?" I asked. "Do they work or just spend their trust funds…as far from you as possible?"

Seriously, his parents had named him *Lord*. Of what? I'd always wondered.

Lord's posse of like-minded bullies pulled him away before he could throw a punch at me. Smart of them, though I wasn't opposed to busting my knuckles, taking a few hits, or even breaking a bone or two. If I did, maybe, *finally* my mom would remember I existed. Maybe my father would stop being so distant.

Nothing had worked since Lev's death—not stellar grades, not the cigarettes or the vaping cartridges I stole from Lord, or even me swilling from a bottle of vodka while sitting on Mom's bed and talking to her last week.

Hugh grunted. "You're pushing it with him. No matter who your parents are, it won't help if Lord and his buddies decide to take you down."

Hugh was a nice kid, and I actually liked spending time with him. He was easygoing and funny, unlike most of the kids here at Holyoke, who I simply couldn't stand to be around.

Lord yanked his arms from his friends' hands and turned to glare at me. Just to piss him off more, I waved. Lord's face darkened, but he strode off.

"I'm not sure I want to take advice from the punk who kissed Naomi after lunch today," I said, turning toward Hugh.

Fear seeped into his features before he stood up straight. "She kissed *me*."

"I know. That's the only reason I haven't pounded *you* into the ground. Except I don't need to hit you to ruin you, and we both know it."

One call—that's all it would take to blackball Lord or Hugh. Not just because my mother, Carolina, had been *the* supermodel when she married my father, and because of that fame, she still had a packed schedule. Or because my father, Brad, was one of the hottest names in rock. Nope. Carolina Syad Porter's father, my Pop Syad, had more money than most countries. His bank account made us Porters look like paupers.

"You wouldn't," Hugh said, eyes wide.

"You remember what an obnoxious little shit I was in elementary school," I said. That was part of the reason I didn't hate on Hugh, even after today's incident. I'd known him since kindergarten—and he'd been nice to me after Lev died.

"But that was before. And since, you know, your brother died, you've been…"

Fucked up. I was so fucked up. If Lev hadn't drowned in the lake behind our house last year, maybe my mom wouldn't have turned to substances and my dad to pounding anything with a vagina to forget their shared pain.

Their vices left me unable to move forward and unwilling to fall back—a terrible limbo I'd been stuck in so long it felt… if not normal then *conventional.* And I *hated* this conventional space I existed in.

Hugh continued to meet my gaze, his irises too dark, but it was my insides that were black around the edges. Hugh was from a relatively normal family—if any family that lived among the sprawling homes and ranches dotting the Hill Country could be considered normal. I didn't think they could—not after I'd turned on the news a couple of months ago and caught the latest crazy-town events happening at the house next to ours, where Camden Grace lived.

Cam was a rising star in the music world, and I'd met him two years ago at a music festival where my dad first played the song I'd created. Cam had performed a stage over from my dad's band, and I'd soaked up his edgy sound and deep, dark Springsteen-like lyrics. When Cam found out who I was—from his security chief, Chuck—he'd invited Lev and me to hang out backstage. Lev had been into a girl, and more interested in following her around, but I stayed with Cam for a few hours and learned that he lived in my neighborhood back in Texas.

He'd invited me to jam with him a few times after that, but

slammed into the side of my head, filling my mouth with water and knocking me into the sand.

I struggled to rise, even as another wave slammed into me. I clenched the shell and curled up smaller, afraid to rise again. Then, the boy's hand grasped mine and pulled. When I stumbled, he tugged me again, harder. I gasped and coughed out water as I managed to get to my feet. He led me from the ocean. I collapsed on my bottom near my sandcastle, sucking in air.

"They didn't see," he muttered, glancing over his shoulder at my parents. "That's why I came over. My mommy said it's not safe."

I blinked up at him. "For me?" I asked.

He squatted next to me, and I was able to see his eyes. They were a warm, soft brown—a little darker than the liquor my daddy put in his glass each night. The outer rims were dark, almost as black as his pupils.

"For kids," he said. "How old are you?"

"I'm five."

"Same as me." He smiled. "I'm glad you didn't drown. That's a bad thing to do. We only get to live on the water as long as we follow the rules."

"My dad's being mean," I whispered.

He frowned. "Mine makes my mommy cry."

I gazed at him, both liking and hating that we had this in common. "I don't like when my mummy cries."

"Why do you say 'mummy' like that?" He sat on his heels, his knees tucked into his blue swim trunks.

"My dad's English." I shrugged.

I settled my perfect conch on his knee. My skin felt hot, and

I couldn't hold his gaze, so I rubbed my wet legs into the sand, coating them in the fine, white powder. I peeked at him. He was studying me, not the shell.

"You're pretty," he said.

"So are you," I replied.

He grinned, and a dimple appeared in his rounded left cheek. "Yeah, I am. My mommy's the most beautiful-est lady in the world. She says I look like her. But she doesn't have purple eyes like yours."

Something about this boy made it hard for me to find my words.

He snatched up the shell and stood. "Thanks."

He turned and trotted back toward his mother, who'd started to walk this direction from another of the large blue umbrellas. Hers was halfway down the beach, in front of the largest villa. She wore a large, black hat and large sunglasses. Her pale skin glistened, and her one-piece swimsuit was cut higher on the legs and lower across the chest than my mum's. Her bright red lips turned up in a smile as the boy approached her.

"What's your name?" I called.

He stopped about halfway between us. "Nash. Nash Porter, and one day I'm going to be a superstar."

He darted to his mother and lifted the shell he cradled in his hands. She admired it, patting his head before moving off once more. He followed, seeming to trip over his feet in an effort to keep her attention.

Nash Porter.

I watched him walk away, the hand that had held the conch now sitting over my hammering heart.

Chapter 2

SEVEN YEARS LATER

Nash

Screams ripped through my noise-canceling headphones, making me wince—in the best possible way. I rocked back on my heels, awed by the power of twenty-thousand people cheering for my dad's band, Quantum.

As the band hit the opening riff, a rush of adrenaline flowed through me, and my fingertips tingled. As the guitars sang through the early measures, my chest throbbed in time with the beat.

Then, Dad began to sing *my* lyrics. Sweat dripped from his brow, and his long bangs stuck to his forehead. He shot me a wink.

Our little secret, it said.

I grinned back. *Oh yeah.* As long as I got to come along and see this response to my music, I was more than happy to stay back here. For now. Bieber had been thirteen, a year older than me, when he stormed the world stage. But as my dad had pointed out, he'd made some bad choices along the way.

"*Enjoy being a kid, Nash. It doesn't last long,*" he'd said with his hand on my shoulder, gripping it in that comforting way of his before the *pat, pat, pat* on my back.

The screaming grew to a crescendo.

"Not a bad response, little bro," Lev said, slinging his arm around my shoulder.

I beamed. He laughed, his voice cracking halfway through it, then he had a groupie break into his place and burn the house to the ground. His leaving had coincided with Lev's death last year, so I'd lost my brother *and* my pseudo-friend/mentor.

That left me with Hugh.

Hugh was taller than me now, with dark hair to go with his tawny complexion. His plastic-surgeon dad was Greek or Haitian or something—I'd never bothered to ask because it didn't matter, really. The important detail was that Hugh never pushed me about my mom or my brother. *That's* why I let him stick around.

And now, as Hugh continued to hold my gaze, even knowing that I'd expressed interest in Naomi, I gave him mad props for the show of bravery.

"Like I said, she kissed *me*, and I like her back," Hugh said. "Like, *a lot.* So take someone else."

"Or what?" I asked, my voice soft. Naomi was pretty and fun. I liked the idea of kissing her, but to *like* her the way Hugh seemed to? No, I wasn't that stupid.

Hugh swallowed, his Adam's apple bobbing. "Or I'll quit hanging out with you." His voice cracked and then broke.

I studied him. "You'd do that—over a *girl*?" I asked.

For a moment, Hugh's resolve dimmed, and I thought I'd broken him, but then he straightened. "Yeah. For Naomi I would."

I shrugged, even as I wondered if I'd ever like a girl enough to forfeit a friendship. After seeing my parents' implosion, I doubted I'd ever even bother with a girlfriend.

I wondered if I'd ever have another friend, a *true* one, like Lev had been. Like Cam had tried to be.

I wondered about a lot of things during ninth grade, especially since I cut myself off from Hugh after that day and didn't have much of anyone else to talk to.

But that was all before I met her.

Well, *met* might've been too strong a word. I *heard* about the new chick when our English teacher informed us of a lame-ass project that was supposed to help us with those all-important communication skills.

I grimaced. I didn't need to work on stupid English syntax. I needed to write a hit song so my dad would look at me with pride and excitement again. So we could be a family.

"We've been asked to set up a pen-pal relationship with an incoming student," Ms. Gates, our English teacher, explained. "She's currently in Nepal with her mother. When Aya Aldringham returns to the United States, she'll attend Holyoke." Ms. Gates said this with glee, which led me to believe this Aya chick's family was loaded and had been very, very generous in their giving. "And we can all agree that it'll be nice for her to have friends."

I rolled my eyes, already hating on this rich girl, gaming the system.

"Each of you will send Aya an email, as she's quite anxious about joining our class," Ms. Gates said.

I snorted. No way, no how.

"Here's a picture of her."

I glanced up at the smart board where Aya's picture bloomed on the white space. As soon as I saw those eyes peering out from all that smooth, tanned skin, my mouth went dry. I *knew* those eyes. A memory wormed its way to the surface: a girl with a shy smile, a wave, white sand…the shell I still kept on my nightstand.

A buzzing started in my ears. I couldn't look away from those thickly lashed eyes. Those eyes mesmerized me.

They were purple. No, not purple. I continued to study them. A more bluish tone near her pupil that radiated out into… Hell, I took art. What was that color called? *Violet.* Yeah. The chick's—*Aya's*—eyes were violet. The shade was even more striking against her dark hair.

And they were soft, filled with knowing—like she understood how hard it was to be the rich, famous kid. Like she *cared* that my brother was dead, that my only friend, Hugh, had chosen a girl over me, and that my buddy Cam was busy living his life—and not interested in the fact that my mom cried herself to sleep every night.

Maybe Aya did understand all that. Maybe. I mean, her parents hadn't even realized she'd been so close to danger all those years ago. I'd dragged her out of the waves—something I hadn't been able to do for my brother. But that little girl…I'd saved her. And she'd looked up at me like I was the most heroic person ever.

I *loved* that feeling.

I'd wanted to see her again, had thought of her for weeks after that happened.

And now, the soft sound of waves filled my head, followed by the wind instruments from Claude Debussy's *La Mer*. Shock rippled down my spine. I didn't hear music that way anymore, yet the song flowed through my mind. The girl, the song… I shook myself. Literally. Like a dog flinging off excess water.

"I guess that disruption was to draw attention to yourself. Thank you for volunteering, Mr. Porter," Ms. Gates said, her smile more of a sneer.

I never paid attention and still managed to get As. My ability to do so drove Ms. Gates batty, which was why she was always looking for reasons to give me extra work or make me look bad.

She waddled to my desk, iPad in hand. "Type out a note right now. That way I'll know you did it."

I rolled my eyes, which landed on the icon of Aya Aldringham. Her eyes seemed to comfort me even from the tiny picture.

I took a deep breath as I typed.

Hey, Aya,

I'm in what would be your English class in your grade at Holyoke School, aka School for Rich and Bored Deviants. Ms. Gates asked me to tell you a bit about the class, which sucks—and the school, which is okay but not really hard—so you'll be more comfortable when you show up.

I bit my lip, remembering Ms. Gates saying the girl had anxiety. I could at least attempt to alleviate her worries.

Mostly, the kids establish a pecking order, and you hang out with people in your tier. Stick with me, kid, and you'll be top-tier.

Why was I being so honest?

I needed to delete everything I'd written and start over.

The bell rang before I had a chance, and Ms. Gates plucked the device from my hands, tutting as she read what I'd written. I made a grab for it, but she pressed send before I could highlight and delete it.

"Now you've scared the poor girl," Ms. Gates said, a malicious gleam in her eye.

Oh, this all made sense. She'd asked me to write something so she could get me in trouble with the head of school. As if a mark in my record would get me kicked out. Still, I didn't want to disappoint my parents or my grandfather. They had enough going on already. No way this lumbering teacher was going to give my mother another reason to drink or get high.

"I wasn't finished typing," I said, snatching the iPad from her chubby claws and darting into the hall before she could catch me. I hustled out the side door and leaped over a low fence, tugging my phone from my pocket even as I tucked the iPad under my arm.

I pressed the first entry in my speed dial for Steve, my driver/bodyguard. Pop Syad had sent Steve home with me after Lev's funeral. My guess was my grandfather expected the former soldier to keep me safe. I wished Lev had had a Steve shadow. Then maybe he'd still be alive.

"Meet me on the west side, under the big tree."

I hung up before he could respond. I tore around the lacrosse field, backpack smacking my back as I tucked the iPad into my T-shirt. I shoved the tail into my jeans just as I made a running leap for the edge of the seven-foot wrought-iron fence, which I scaled with ease thanks to years of parkour.

I hit the ground with an ankle-jarring thud and glanced back, my breath rushing from my lungs. Ms. Gates was nowhere to be seen.

Good. I had time to correct the message by sending a second one that made Ms. Gates look bad. No way the squinty-eyed hag would jeopardize her cushy position at one of the premier private schools in the nation once I sent Aya my version of what had gone down in the classroom today.

I chuckled.

There was no point in just getting back at Ms. Gates, or anyone else.

I always preferred to get even.

Chapter 4
Nash

The lyrics from "Gives You Hell" by the All-American Rejects drifted through my head as I stared up at the ceiling of my room. That song annoyed me even as I was thankful to have *something* in my mind again.

Aya had *dismissed* me. I'd saved her life—well, at least pulled her from that big wave—all those years ago, and she didn't have the decency to reply immediately? It had been three full days since my messages to her. I'd followed up that first one with a couple more, trying to explain how she'd ended up with the first one. Maybe she thought I was crazy. *Three freaking days.*

I hated rejection. It gave me a squirmy, dark feeling in my gut. One that reminded me of Lev…

A new message popped up. I narrowed my eyes, but after no more than a moment, the oppressive boredom of being home, alone, in all that space, thinking about my dead brother, made me click on the message. That was the *only* reason. It was from her. *Finally*. Not because I wanted to see if she remembered me, too.

Or if she still thought I was pretty.

Or because I missed Lev.

Or because I needed to talk to someone since I'd not decided on whether to forgive Hugh yet…

The note opened on my screen.

Dear Nash,

I'm totally freaking out about attending Holyoke. Freaking out!

I don't want to meet these atrociously mannered kids, let alone interact with them every day. But my mum said I need Western education. Probably because I've spent most of my life living in the bush in Africa and Asia. In case you didn't know, my mum runs this nonprofit, Clean Water, that's tackling sanitation needs.

We're currently in Nepal. I get to school by climbing the side of a mountain. It'd be a lot cooler if I wasn't terrified of heights. I nearly puke each time.

I don't have social anxiety, though, and I have no idea why the teacher told you that. Maybe because I'm coming from a foreign country, and I told her I was anxious about the books you're reading and what you're studying in history, math, and science. Send me some details, please?

I only get messages on my phone when I climb to the top of the mountain. Write back soon—don't make me climb up here for nothing.

Your friend,

Aya

PS—I'm glad you think my eyes are pretty. Send me a photo of what you look like.

Huh. This girl sounded genuine. She wouldn't last long once Lord and his crew sank their mean fingers into her. I snapped a shot of myself lying on my denim-covered beanbag chair and sent it to her, along with a laundry list of books we'd read and were supposed to read. I glanced at my overflowing bookshelf, a pang of longing hitting me.

Lev had loved to read, and I'd commandeered most of his books. Maybe Aya had read them, and we could talk about them.

What was *wrong* with me? I didn't like to read. And I didn't chat with chicks.

I shoved thoughts of my brother aside and wrote to Aya about our history assignments and what math and science work we'd been doing.

She replied quickly, stating that I was "cute."

I curled my lip at that.

You look like a boy I met, years ago, while on vacation. He disappeared before I could tell him my name, but I remember his: Nash Porter. Are you that same person, Superstar?

That was a loaded question. I wasn't the kid I'd been on that trip. My family had been cohesive then, and I'd been happy. I'd enjoyed playing the little girl's protector because everyone always babied *me.*

The song in my head faded, but I barely noticed. I was too busy typing…and enjoying myself. Huh. Who would have thought? I hit send, and within moments, she'd responded.

I thought so. What happened to the shell? she asked.

I smirked as I surveyed the expansive space of my room—the beanbags in front of the gaming console, the pale wood that made up my nightstand, the shell atop it, and the intricate yet simple geometric pattern of my headboard. My bed was made, sheets and thin summer duvet tightly tucked against the mattress thanks to our new housekeeper. Dad had fired the previous staff of house help a few months after Lev died—I think when he realized Steve was on Pop Syad's payroll, not his. For some reason,

Steve's presence really pissed Dad off. When Dad lost his shit and started yelling at Mom, she left the house in tears and flew off early for her next commercial.

Still got it, I typed.

Good. It was perfect, she replied after a moment. *I never found another one like it.*

Do you remember anything else from that trip? I asked.

Not really. Just you, Mr. Superstar. And your mom. She was very beautiful.

My mouth smashed flat, and I accidentally took another photo when I squeezed my phone too tight. Worse, I somehow managed to attach it to the message and send it.

No, no, that couldn't happen—she couldn't see *that.* I looked like a moron.

Whatever. She was just some random girl. I didn't need to impress her. I didn't need to impress anyone.

What's wrong? Why the world-weary face?

My breath trickled out of my lungs as tension seeped from my shoulders. Good. She wasn't going to be a dick about my mistake. Huh. She really was nice.

And her assessment was one I agreed with, even liked. I'd traveled the world, and I was weary. Damn tired of my parents' inability to pull their heads out of their asses about Lev's death and remember they had a living, breathing kid still at home who'd totally lick up even scraps of their time and attention.

I pressed send before I realized I'd been typing my thoughts.

I stared at the email, aghast. I hadn't meant to send her that much truth.

Holy *shit.*

"Hit Me With Your Best Shot" sprang to life into my head. I tried and failed to enjoy it because anxiety wormed through my guts, leaving me feeling perforated.

I'd sent this chick I didn't know my entire life story, all the details I'd never, ever tell anyone here. The kids would use it against me, hurt me. *Berate* me. Rip me apart.

I dropped my phone and sank my fingers into my hair.

What was happening to me? I'd been so sure I'd lost the ability to hear music, and yet the moment I saw Aya's picture, it had begun to come back. Now, even as I freaked out about this girl who probably wasn't as nice as she pretended to be, songs ran rampant through my mind.

My heart pounded so hard, I worried it would burst through my lungs. Hearing music was good—no, *great*! I couldn't wait to tell my dad about its return, but…the email. I was an idiot, and I *had* to get it back. I *had* to stop her from reading it—a new message popped up.

Aya must still be standing atop the mountain, gathering the courage to head back down. Well, that's if what she'd told me about her life thus far was true. How would I know? And why should I believe her, just because she said it was so?

I pondered her weird story and how I'd do with climbing up and down rocks to get to class or to talk to someone on the other side of the world.

If they can't get past their loss, then they're losing again, her message said. *They're losing you!*

You seem like a really great guy, Nash. The little boy I met was very sweet, and I can tell he's still in you. I'm so glad, because I was worried you were one of those cynical mean kids.

My mum and I started traveling when my parents divorced. It was ugly—the divorce, not the travel. I miss what my family was like when everyone got along, but I barely remember that time. My dad hates talking to my mum, so he avoids me, too. Now he has a new family, and he seems happier than I remember him. Happier now that I'm not around.

Poor Aya. Her dad had basically replaced her because he couldn't stand her mom. *Ugly*. Yeah, that word held a world of fights, silences, and heartbreak.

Grownups could be such petty shits. I told Aya so but got no response. She'd probably started climbing down the freaking Himalayas.

Oh, and I want to see your view, I typed. *Do one of those real-time panos so I get the sound of wind and the birds and all that.*

I'd catch her in a lie if she didn't send it, and then I could ignore her. No one would believe her if she decided to share my story. I'd say I'd been hacked.

But if she was telling the truth…well, then this Aya chick was badass. And sweet.

I dug the sweetness in her replies for some reason, maybe because she reminded me of my mom before Lev's death. I missed her—*that* mom, the one who told me often how much she cared, who showed it in her hugs and by carving out time for me every single day.

As bad as my situation was, I knew my parents still cared about my well-being. My dad brought me into the studio off of

Sixth Street for jam sessions, and my mom hugged me when she came home, which was less and less frequent the more she and Dad fought.

So, the problem wasn't *me*. Like Lev said, there'd long been an unequal balance of success in our family. And it was the heavy blanket of grief and my parents' inability to communicate with each other. This caused tension between them and left me emotionally raw and unsure.

That's what the therapist I saw every Wednesday said, anyway, and my parents had both agreed with her when we visited together again for the second time last month. Mom and Dad were just overwhelmed. Tired.

The situation wasn't my fault.

But it was—at least some of it. Maybe if I'd written that song Dad wanted, he and Mom wouldn't have been fighting that night, and Lev would still be alive.

I locked my jaw, wishing I'd been able to compose something—even a shit jingle Dad could have screwed around with—to save my family.

Much as I wanted to believe the shrinks and my parents, Lev's death still felt like my fault.

I wanted to tell Aya that, too, but I wouldn't. Sharing those secrets was foolhardy.

Because email was too slow, I clicked on the number she'd listed in her signature and exited the school email account. I brought up my text app. I sent her a message, and she replied.

Yes, this is me. Hang on. I'm trying to do the panorama.

A moment later, my text app chimed again, and I opened a

slow video of the most rugged, beautiful country I'd ever seen. My jaw dropped.

It's beautiful. Why would you want to leave that?

My mother said we'll leave when Clean Water wraps up the sanitation project.

Show me those handholds and how you get down, I wrote.

She sent the picture, and once again, my jaw dropped. I squinted, trying to make out any place to grip.

This girl was definitely badass.

What time is it there? I asked.

It's about seven in the morning. I have to get back down to help feed the sheep.

I laughed. I was talking to freaking Heidi, the sheepherder. Except this girl's parents were wealthy enough to stay at the same exclusive bungalows in Turks and Caicos that my family had stayed in, and her dad was some kind of British lord or something. At least, that's what Ms. Gates had said during English class.

I went downstairs, unsurprised to find Steve in the living room. He was former Army and told me he'd seen some serious action during his multiple tours in Iraq and then Afghanistan. Even when he was still, he gave off this air of faint menace. Or it could've been his light eyes that never remained still. They were always narrowed enough to make me think he could actually *see* my evil thoughts. He was taller than my dad by a good three or four inches and thicker through the shoulders, chest, and arms. He got up every morning at five a.m. and ran seven to ten miles, which was probably why he looked twenty years younger than my dad, even though he was in his early thirties to my dad's forties.

"What's up?" Steve asked, looking up from a crossword puzzle. His pale eyes assessed me. His blond hair had grown out from the buzz to a conservative cut, and his face was cleanly shaven, showing off a deep chin dimple.

"Apparently we're going to get a new kid at school. I've been wondering about her."

He raised his eyebrows. "And?"

"I'm sure you know about her. I want to, too."

"Why do you think I know anything?"

I rolled my eyes. "Because Pop Syad pays you to protect me. So I'm guessing you know way more about the new girl than I do."

Steve shrugged. "I might know something. And you're right. I don't like surprises. They can create chaos."

I snorted. "That's all high school is—social chaos masquerading as education."

Steve's eyes gleamed, but he kept his expression stern. "If you want my intel on the new girl, then you're going to tell me why I had to pick you up from the side of the school the other day. And I want to know what *that* has to do with the irate phone calls your mother is fielding from Ms. Gates."

I waved my hand. "That woman hates me, and it has to do with the new kid." I considered my options. Steve could get me the information I wanted—if I played nice.

"Ms. Gates asked me to write a note, but then she took the iPad from me before I finished typing. I grabbed it back, and then I had to get to a quiet place." I shrugged, hoping he was buying this. "So I could actually tell the girl more about the school."

He went back to his crossword puzzle. "Aya is Lord Reginald Aldringham's daughter, and Irwan Didri's granddaughter. Your grandfather was the one to recommend Holyoke to her grandfather."

I scowled, displeased that Steve knew the answers even as I soaked up the information.

"And?"

"And nothing," he said with a shrug. "What do you want for dinner?"

He'd been making me dinner lately, or at least making sure I ate whatever our personal chef left.

"I want to know more about the girl."

Steve cocked his head to the side. "Why?"

I licked my lower lip. "I met her before. Years ago. And she seems nice."

Steve nodded once. "You can tell me more over dinner, and then, once you do your homework, I'll get you some intel."

Chapter 5

ONE YEAR LATER

Nash

A year passed, and Aya and I now chatted on the regular. She'd never left Nepal—something to do with a problem with the village wells—but she caught up on enough celebrity news even on the top of a mountain to know my parents' marriage was falling apart.

My dad cheated on my mum, Aya told me in one text after I confirmed that my dad was traveling whenever my mother was home, and she took off when he was expected back.

He didn't ask for the divorce until Harriet fell pregnant, though.

At least neither of my parents had surprise kids out there. I told Aya as much.

I have two half-sisters. And my dad tried to get my mum to pay him alimony.

I felt my eyes widen. *I don't know what to say.*

You don't have to say anything. I just wanted you to know that I get how it feels. And how horrible it is when others ask you about your parents' public breakup.

Because I was still only sometimes speaking to Hugh, Aya was my *only* real friend—not that I was ever lonely. People were always hanging around, hanging on, wanting a piece of me, and inviting me to more parties and events than I could manage.

I turned down most in order to talk to Aya or to hang out with

Cam, who had returned to Austin to help out at his family's ranch located at the edge of Hill Country. I liked Cam's sister, Kate, and mother, Mama Grace. She and Steve got along well and at least partially filled the large hole my parents left with their neglect.

I hadn't shared the pathetic truth of our friendship truth with Aya, not wanting her to think less of me, though Cam had disagreed last time we'd video chatted. He might technically live in the same city as me, but the guy toured constantly.

"You should tell Aya she's important to you," Cam said.

I raised an eyebrow. "No way. You know how this world is. I'll say something that'll end up in a magazine."

He frowned. "You think this girl would sell you out?"

I didn't. But I wasn't willing to offer her the opportunity either.

Cam called me again a couple nights later, after I'd chatted with Aya. The dude kept in better touch with me than my parents.

"You want to hear who I collaborated with today?" he asked instead.

"Sure."

"Asher Smith."

"Are you for real?" I asked, sitting up straight. "Is he badass in real life?"

Cam laughed. "Yes, he is. He's offered to help produce my next record. What do you think about this riff?

I closed my eyes as Cam played, my fingers moving over a phantom fretboard. The rest of the melody soared through my mind when Cam stopped, mentioning he didn't have it finished.

I dove toward my guitar and continued playing. The song…

It ran through my head, faster than my fingers could move over the strings. The melody built, richer, as more instruments flitted through my mind.

"And you need to add something softer—a harp, maybe? Then the piano chords should be..." I pursed my lips, trying to figure out how to translate from the guitar to the keyboard. "I'll send it to you," I said, feeling myself smile. This was it. *I'd written a song.*

Cam shook his head. He pulled a candy from his pocket and slid it into his mouth. He had a thing for Werther's. "You just come up with that?"

"Yeah."

"What's your dad say about your ability to compose?"

That feeling wrapped itself around my guts as sadness punched me in the throat. It must have shown on my face.

"Nash—"

"It's all in the family," I blurted out over Cam, not wanting to hear more sympathetic words. My brother was dead—had been for a while now. I needed to move on. I *was* moving beyond the crippling grief.

My comment to Cam had once been Dad's favorite comment to me. "*All in the family.*" He'd slapped me on the shoulder whenever I played him a new tune, and I'd beamed with pride when my dad used my songs on his albums. *All in the family* was right. Or it used to be.

"What?" Cam asked.

"Music, composing. It's our thing. We do it together."

Cam's eyes narrowed. "You help him with his songs?"

"Yeah, sure."

Cam grimaced. "His last album?"

I nodded.

"I've never seen you credited."

I shrugged. "I was young."

"What about the album he's working on?"

That feeling intensified, causing my guts to harden. I hadn't been able to write shit since before Lev died—until today. "Nope, that's all him."

Cam grunted, eyes narrowing.

"I gotta go," I said, not wanting to discuss the topic further.

"You sure you're good there?" Cam asked, concern darkening his gaze.

The guy was twenty-nine, and he seemed much older in my mind because he worried so much about me. The groupie thing and losing his house a couple of years ago had made him "rethink his priorities," he'd told me. He'd said being a good person—and a good friend to me, apparently—sat at the top of his list now.

"I'm cool."

Cam remained tense.

I cleared my throat, not liking the emotions building in me. "I'll record that melody and send it to you. But I don't play the harp—"

"Yet," Cam said, chuckling.

My cheeks burned. "I don't play the harp," I insisted. "So, you'll have to get someone else to fine-tune that bit."

"Of course." He nodded. "It's not like I expect you to write my songs. You know you're a lot more to me than anything you can do, right, son?"

"Yeah, sure," I said. I strummed the guitar.

"But I do appreciate what you did tonight."

"It felt good."

"Why haven't you been composing music?"

That was a loaded question. I just…didn't. Maybe *couldn't* was a better response. The only flickers of lyrics or snippets of songs that came at all came when I was texting with Aya or talking with Cam.

I didn't want to tell him that, so I shrugged.

He sighed. "I'll be back in town at the end of the week. How about I pick you up? We can head to the studio. Sound good?"

My eyes widened. "Really? Yeah. I'd like that."

Cam smiled. "I already told Asher about you. He's stoked."

"Cool," I gushed.

I set my guitar in its stand and brushed the hair out of my eyes. "I mean…that's nifty."

Cam smirked as he shook his head. "Well, you can meet him sometime if you want. I'm sure he'd like that. You're close in age to his son."

At my gulp, Cam guffawed.

I clicked off before I could embarrass myself any more.

I messed around with the melody a little after that, mainly because I had nothing better to do. Aya hadn't answered my texts for the last couple of days. Much as I hated to admit it, I was mad. Mad and…hurt.

Aya's messages had helped me navigate my parents' boozy, mainly silent holidays, as well as their long absences. I'd sent her tons of pictures from that last tour I did with my dad and Lev, and she'd asked lots of questions about the music industry and performing, clearly fascinated by the lifestyle.

That's so different than my life here, she'd written at one point. *I mean, I get the nomadic lifestyle. Mum and I usually move every year or so.*

I hadn't thought about that part of her life—the constant need to make new friends, to start over in a new place. When I asked her about it, she told me she'd stopped trying for deep relationships.

You have me, I wrote. *I'll always be here for you.*

Until you get too famous, Superstar. Then you'll be the one touring, living the life of a nomad.

That had made me smile, and Dad had told me next time Quantum toured—later this coming summer—he'd let me play with him, let me tell the world I'd written the music and lyrics.

"*You'll be a man, Nash. You won't need me to protect you from the world, then,*" he'd said. "*But you're still too young. Give it some time.*"

I didn't want to give it any more time.

Yeah, but I think I'll love the constant traveling and performing, I'd replied to Aya. *It's what I'm meant to do.*

All through our sophomore year, from thousands of miles away, Aya talked me out of skipping school when Lord became an even bigger bullying asshole, and she was the reason I turned in most of my assignments. The year slid past, and I did better than anticipated, and our junior year soon melted into the following spring.

Aya had informed me that she'd read every single one of the books on the school's list—so I read them, too, to give us something else to talk about. Not that I was bored talking to Aya. I was never bored around her, which was weird because the girls at school talked about nail polish and shoes. All. The. Time.

And that shit was boring.

Not Aya, though. She was real, deep—like the ocean I'd pulled her from. She was also pretty and delicate like the conch shell she'd given me.

I'd never intended to use her as a sounding board. But it was so easy to send a text when I was anxious or upset or my mother was passed out again. And Aya listened.

Or rather, she checked her messages about twice a week and then would shoot back replies to every message I'd sent, in the order I'd sent them.

By now, I'd collected thousands of messages from Aya Aldringham.

How come you don't mention other friends, Nash? She'd asked in one of her recent ones.

As had become my habit, I answered, not as careful with my words as I used to be. What could Aya do to me? She lived in Nepal. None of the other kids at Holyoke talked to her, and she'd mentioned that her mom now planned to stick around to help the neighboring villages, so ever attending the same school seemed less likely.

Because friends require work, I told her. *Being honest. And the world we live in here isn't about honesty. Or friendship. It's about taking care of yourself.*

I could practically hear the sigh in her response. *You're really selling the city and the hellscape of private school.*

It's not all bad. You'll have me, I wrote.

Ha. You mean you'll use me.

I'd never use you, Aya. I know how important trust is.

I hope so. Because I don't want to be around another guy who lies and cheats and hurts people.

Like your dad? I asked.

And yours.

My dad isn't that bad.

Really? So he's not trying to get you to write more songs for him and then freezing you out when you don't?

He doesn't freeze me out. He's just mad that I helped Camden Grace and not him.

So, when was the last time you and your dad hung out?

I clamped my lip between my teeth. That was the thing about Aya. She saw my situation for what it was. I still had this stupidity about wanting to get along with my dad, which would allow me to pretend everything was better than it was.

Sorry, that was unnecessarily mean, Aya typed after I didn't respond. *When does your father leave for his next tour?*

Dunno. He hasn't finished the album, and the execs are breathing down his neck. I think that's why he's been so pissed—not just at me, but the world. I totally get why my mom's not around. She's trying to flood her liver in an effort to ignore the embarrassment of my dad's other women.

Is that working?

I snorted before I typed. *Considering she's been 'on location' for the past three weeks? Even the media is sure she's refusing to come home at this point. So no. Not even close.*

I guess I'm glad my parents got divorced then.

Yeah. Yeah, that would be better, I wrote.

Chapter 6
Nash

Toward the end of my junior year, when the next February rolled around, Aya sent me a message: *Happy birthday!*

It's tomorrow, I typed back.

I'd been wallowing in my room, frustrated that Cam had a gig and Aya remained impossible to get a hold of. I slammed my head back against the beanbag and shut my eyes, remembering what birthdays used to look like: huge cakes with sparkling candles, streamers, balloons, and laughter.

I missed the laughter.

I missed my mom, and the hurt inside me grew because my father hadn't bothered to suggest we hang out on the deck—our birthday tradition.

Just then he stuck his head into my room. "You got a song for me?" he asked, as he had each of the last few times I'd seen him.

I swallowed the ache building in my chest, the weight of the anxiety pressing against my lungs. "No."

He glared. "What are you doing?"

"Going to school, and—" *And tomorrow's my birthday.*

"I hear you banging around on your instruments. Look, I *need* a hit. If we don't finish this album, we'll have to postpone the tour again. And that's not going to make the label happy."

I bit my lip, ducking my head. Besides the song I'd helped

Cam with more than a year ago, I hadn't heard much in the way of music. I'd looked it up and learned that grief and stress could impact my ability to focus. But I hadn't mentioned the issue to anyone, shame building hard and hot each time my dad didn't come home.

It was almost as if he only cared about my ability to compose music.

My phone chimed, and I sighed out a breath, thankful for the distraction.

Of course I remember. You're about to be seventeen! Aya wrote.

"Are you even listening to me?" my father asked, stepping into the room.

I tensed, his tone as dark as his expression.

"Yeah. I just…"

"Get your head out of your ass, Nash. This, the music, is important. It's what pays for your cushy life."

I opened my mouth, then closed it, unsure what to say. Steve appeared in the doorway.

"Your car's out front, Mr. Porter."

"Fine. Great." Dad turned back to focus on me. "Remember what I said. You need to bring something to the studio on Friday."

Friday? I had school.

Steve frowned too, his gaze remaining on my dad a moment longer than left any of us comfortable.

Dad stormed out of the room.

"What was that?" I asked.

Steve scowled. "I believe your father's feeling some pressure.

From the studio."

"But…why?"

Steve shook his head.

Nash? Did you get my text? Happy 17th birthday!

Aya's text pulled me out of the dark place. Right. Focus.

"You okay, son?" Steve asked.

I nodded, unsure what else to say or do, so I refocused on my phone.

Just remember I'm older, I typed, smiling.

By ten whole days.

I could feel the sarcasm vibrating off her message, which caused my smile to grow.

I'm older, and I saved your life.

Yes, yes, my knight in shining armor. A king among men. Blah, blah, blah.

I barked out a laugh. She actually wrote *blah blah blah*. This girl. She had a fantastic sense of humor.

The next day passed as the previous ones had. I made it through the school day—chatted up by a ton of kids and not interested in any of them. I wished Aya was here, with me. I wished my mother would come home. I didn't want to celebrate my birthday alone. Again.

So, I was more than a bit relieved to receive a text from Aya late that afternoon. It had to be really early in Nepal, and the fact that she'd woken up and climbed the side of the mountain, for me, made me smile.

Got any plans for the big b-day? she asked.

Not really.

But I knew Aya had already surmised as much, which was why she'd made the climb two days in a row. Warmth spread through my chest. This girl—this girl I hadn't even seen since we were five, meant more to me than just about anyone in my life.

You know what I want, more than anything? Aya wrote.

No idea.

Cats. Well, kittens. I want a bunch of sweet furry babies to cuddle.

I wouldn't mind a sweet little furball to snuggle with either. Something to love me, to keep me company when my parents weren't here.

Yeah, I'd be down with a kitten, I wrote.

Aya sent a smiley face with heart eyes, making my insides warm. Jeez. I should stop talking to her, but before I set down my phone, another text popped up.

I wanted to ask my mum for one now that we're moving back to 'civilization', but, from what you've told me, I should ask for a car.

Wait, what?? *You're really coming back this time?*

That's what she said.

She's said that before, I wrote.

She seems serious.

Well, then cars are important to teenagers here.

No one here drives.

That's weird.

She sent a shrug emoji.

Tell you what, I'll teach you to drive and get you a cat one day.

And I'll get you one. We'll have twin cats.

We continued to text, and my mood improved even more.

Who cared that my dad was pissed at me? Who cared that he'd probably bang another groupie, causing my mother to party harder in an effort to show she didn't care? Who cared that my mother had been spotted by the paparazzi two hours ago in a posh club off Sunset in LA, sucking down lemon drop martinis like they were water instead of coming home to spend my birthday with me?

I had Aya, and she cared about me.

"Nash!"

I startled out of the version of "Nantucket Sleigh Ride" that included a full orchestra backing up the sweet seventies guitar licks.

I blinked, shocked to find my room dark. How long had I been in here? "Yeah?"

"You got a delivery," Steve called.

I bounded down the stairs, smiling when I saw the balloons and cake box held in the delivery person's arms.

"You Nash Porter?" the bored guy asked.

"Sure am."

The delivery man shoved the box at me, followed by the balloons. "Enjoy."

I set the cake box in the kitchen, pulling off the note.

Happy birthday, honey. We'll celebrate when I get home. This project is wrapping up, and I'll be back soon.

All my love,

Mom

I considered dumping the cake in the trash, but then I opened it. The icing looked rich and chocolatey, so I cut myself a thick slice. The inside was marbled chocolate and butterscotch—the same cake my mom used to order for me when I was little.

Steve walked in and settled in the seat across from me. He slid a large, rumpled package toward me. It appeared as much tape as wrapping paper, but the sight of it made me grin.

"For me?"

"Yeah."

I set my fork down and tore into the paper. I gasped, my gaze flying to his. "You remembered?"

"You said it made a cool sound." He cleared his throat. "If you don't like it…"

I rounded the table and nearly hugged him. At the last moment, I held out my fist, which he bumped with his. "I've always wanted a theremin," I told him, "especially after hearing it on Jack White's 'Missing Pieces.' This is epic." I turned it over, grinning hard.

"Oh, and something else came for you."

Steve brought over an envelope. It was stained with what looked like raindrops. The handwriting was small, neat, a bit loopy.

Everything in me paused as I caught the return address. *Nepal.* Aya had sent me mail. We'd never crossed the line into written missives. But her doing this for me… I blew out a breath.

Steve settled into the chair and crossed his arms. I slit the top of the envelope, trying not to show him my shaking hands.

I pulled out a card. It was a plain white one, no embellishments.

Nash,

We don't have cards here like in the States. But I wanted to wish you happy birthday the old-fashioned way. I ordered you tickets to the

Asher Smith concert, which I'll forward to you next time I'm on the mountain. I know he's your favorite.

Hugs,

Aya

I gaped at the card. "Holy…"

"What?" Steve asked.

My smile widened. "We're going to see Asher Smith. Aya got me tickets."

Steve raised his eyebrow. "Couldn't you have gotten tickets through your dad's record label?"

I shook my head. "Dad doesn't like Asher. I guess something went down between them when I was little. Anyway, no way he'd ask for tickets." I smiled. "But now I *have* to go. Because Aya got them for me."

And because it would rub my dad's face in it a little. Couldn't be sorry about that. Not at all.

The weight of my confrontation with him yesterday hit me again. He'd never pressured me like that before.

"So those are from Aya? The pen pal?" Steve asked.

"Yeah. She's great."

"Is she pretty?"

I nodded, my throat tight. I hesitated a moment before I brought up the most recent photo she'd sent me. She was standing next to a pony, her hand on its neck. Her long, dark hair was tied back in a braid that draped over her shoulder and chest.

The V-neck of her T-shirt showed the top swells of a fabulous set of tits. Thanks to my mother's profession, I'd seen my fair share of scantily clad ladies, and Aya put them all to shame.

I turned my phone around and set it down.

Steve picked it up and studied her for a minute. He looked up at me. "She's *very* pretty."

She had sweet, pink lips I wanted to taste. Lips that I'd bet molded to mine perfectly. I wanted to suck her plump lower one into my mouth and nibble on it. I wanted to do a lot more than that, actually. I'd been fantasizing about getting with Aya since she sent me that first photo—no, since my toad of a ninth-grade English teacher had posted Aya's image on the smart board.

Steve shot me a look, reminding me he'd spoken and I'd nearly fallen into the fantasy of fucking Aya right there in the kitchen.

I swallowed the heaviness of desire. "Yeah. I guess."

Steve shook his head. "Don't fall for a pretty face, Nash."

I snorted. "I'm not going to fall for her. She's in Nepal." *At least for now.* "Plus, I don't do girlfriends."

That was 100% true—much to my female classmates' dismay. I had no interest in taking any of them out. Why should I? Instead I could hang out with Cam and his family, visit my mom on set for a photo shoot or one of her acting roles, or tour with my dad. I'd made out with my fair share of girls during the past couple of years, but I'd never pursued anything more.

I didn't *want* more, especially not if relationships were filled with recriminating glances and stony silences like my parents'. Fuck, neither one of them was even here, at home, for my birthday because they couldn't stand the possibility of running into the other.

"Want a piece?" I asked, attempting to send my mind elsewhere. I hated thinking about my parents.

Steve nodded. "I like cake."

"This one's good," I said as I cut him a slice even bigger than mine.

"Your mom said she's going to call," he told me.

She wouldn't, not now that it was happy hour, but I didn't bother to respond. Just like I didn't bother asking where my dad was.

Didn't matter. I had cake and two of the coolest gifts ever.

Then Cam called to invite me to his family's ranch that weekend for a barbecue.

"We gotta celebrate your birthday," he said. "Wish I could be there sooner."

"You're on tour. You don't need—"

"I want to. Now, can you make it?"

"Yeah, sure."

When we hung up, I smiled. I had Steve and Cam and Cam's family to balance out my self-absorbed parents. Life was good.

I savored every bite of my cake, licking my fork clean.

As I took my plate to the sink, Steve told me his mom used to make him a butterscotch cake with chocolate icing when he was young.

"Cool. Something we have in common," I said. "Great taste in cake."

He paused, bite halfway to his mouth. "Guess so. You're not interested in an actual meal since you ate dessert already, are you?"

I snorted, and he smirked. He knew I'd been a bottomless pit of eating for the past few months, especially since I'd started running with him a few mornings a week.

I'd told him I needed the exercise, but mainly I wanted to feel connected to someone. Steve had never brought it up again, but he always made sure he had the blue sports drink I preferred waiting for me on the counter each morning.

"How about I heat up some of those filet mignons the chef left?" Steve asked. "With those potatoes you like?"

I grinned. "Sounds good. With the creamed spinach. I like that stuff."

Steve tousled my hair. "You're a good kid, Nash."

I nodded at him. "Thanks. You're not bad yourself."

"Why don't you put away the rest of the cake while I get dinner started?"

I slid the cake in the fridge and pounded back up the stairs to grab my phone. I found more texts from Aya and Cam waiting.

I smiled.

Yeah. This birthday did not suck. At all.

Chapter 7
Aya

"Are you nervous?" Mum asked.

I stared down at the pixels that made up Nash's face on my phone. His sun-streaked, light brown hair was messy, thanks to the bit of natural curl I'd detected around his ears. It was long in the front, falling into his warm brown eyes. They were well spaced over his nose, reminding me of the statues I'd seen with my mother when we stopped over in Rome a couple of years ago on our way to England.

I'd had to pay respects to my father's second child with his second wife, and the only good part of the trip had been the art history lesson.

"About what?" I asked. I forced my gaze away from my phone, which I'd turned back on as soon as the pilot rose to cruising altitude. I'd planned to look out at the Himalayas one last time, but leaving Nepal caused a deep ache in my chest. The village had been home for nearly three years. I'd celebrated more birthdays there than anywhere else, including my seventeenth, just two months ago.

"Oh, I don't know. New city, new school, nearly the end of the year, college applications—you pick which one to talk about first."

I stopped tapping my foot on the plush carpet that lined the central aisle of my grandfather's private jet and turned toward my mother. Typically, Mum would've taken a commercial flight, unwilling to spend unnecessary funds on private planes, regardless of the fact that her family owned multiple jets. But this trip was different. I just wasn't sure why.

"I am a little nervous about all the school and social stuff," I admitted. I hesitated, wondering if I should mention my Holyoke pen pal, Nash.

My mother shifted as she grimaced, her breath coming up short.

"What's going on with you?" I asked.

While Mum still maintained her tan, the pallor underneath was becoming more visible. Or I was looking harder for it. Her features were still as beautiful as years before, but her brown eyes lacked their typical sparkle, and her eyelids drooped with exhaustion. Her hair was still thick and jet black, but its previous luster seemed dimmed.

My mother's family was French and Tunisian. Mum liked to tell the story of an "indiscretion" between a French general in the late nineteenth century, not long after the French invaded Tunisia, and a noble family's daughter, which produced a son. Because of the boy's French blood, he eventually emigrated to France where he, my great-grandfather, met a Parisian schoolteacher. They'd raised my grandfather and three more children in a small flat in Paris, and he'd studied medicine at Sorbonne. In the late eighties, my Jeddi bought a bio-medical company in Austin, Texas, and he'd moved my mother and French grandmother there.

He liked the weather and the wide-open spaces, but that didn't mean he'd left behind his heritage or traditions. More of them were instilled within me now that we'd spent the past few years in Nepal, reinforcing the Eastern philosophies Mum said Westerners brushed off.

"I have something for you." She slipped her hand into the pocket of her cardigan and pulled out a black velvet pouch. She held it in her palm.

I stared for a moment before I plucked it from my mum's thin hand. Opening the drawstring, I drew out the small, garnet beads, my thumb tickled by the matching silk tassel.

"Malas?" I asked. "You want me to *meditate*?"

"If you'd like," Mum said. "Or you can say mantras as you were taught in the village."

I stared at the twenty-seven uniform red beads, unsure if I wanted to accept what they represented. I'd enjoyed saying the mantras with the other kids in my classes…for a while. Until I realized they side-eyed me when I spoke their sacred words. *Theirs*, not mine.

It was just like it had been in Kenya, and Mozambique, and Laos. I was tired of participating in cultures I could never fully understand because of being born in London. I hadn't lived in *that* city long enough to remember much about it, but that didn't seem to matter. I was different, thanks to my faint British accent, parentage, and lighter skin.

So, wearing the bracelet felt like co-opting a culture that wasn't mine. Yet I'd lived in Nepal longer than I'd spent in any Western country since toddlerhood.

"I'll help you put it on."

I held out my wrist though my jaw shifted, jutting outward

with the need to balk at my mum's request. My mum wanted this for me. Why, though, I wasn't sure.

"I chose garnet because it enhances creative power," she explained. "It can also help with feelings of abandonment."

I clenched both fists and wrenched my arm back, not caring that the beads slipped from my wrist and pooled on the leather seat between us.

"What's going on?" I asked.

Mum closed her eyes, no doubt unhappy with my acerbic tone. "I need to get back to the US. I need… Let's just do this one step at a time."

She wrapped her fingers around the beads again and reached for my wrist, her long fingers cool against my skin. "Wear it, please. For me."

I pulled my knees up to my chest and wrapped my arms around them, shrugging off my mother's hand once the beads were in place. "I guess you're going to make me go to that stupid rich-kids school, then?"

A thrill went through me, though, because that "stupid" school housed Nash Porter, currently my closest friend after years of corresponding. I had answered him initially out of boredom, but we had grown close through all those messages, and I… Heat spread up my chest and neck, suffusing my face.

I liked him. A lot.

I liked the way he teased me. I liked that I was the first person he contacted when he exited the school building. I liked that he confided details of his life that he didn't dare tell others. Like that he, too, wanted a cat. Or about how his dad was riding him hard about composing new songs. I knew his favorite cake and that his musical hero was Asher Smith. I knew he lived near Jeddi's mansion and that he hated to drive but had promised to teach me.

"Yes. You need an education, and it's the best school in the area," Mum said after a moment. "Your grandfather insisted."

I rolled my eyes. "Fine." But the idea of seeing Nash in person caused my stomach to dip, swoop, and realign with giddiness. Then I touched the smooth, red beads with trepidation. How long would I get to spend with Nash before Mum and I moved again?

I released a tiny sigh. No, no more moving. After this, I wouldn't have to make new friends, and I wouldn't have to learn how to navigate a new town. In fifteen months, I would graduate from high school. Then I planned to attend a nearby university known for its engineering program. While I didn't love the idea of living in a large city, I did love the idea of settling in. And now I could make my own choice.

This move—or the next, to college—would be my last. Austin, Texas, was now my home.

Chapter 8
Nash

Aya appeared at Holyoke one morning in April—with just six weeks left in our junior year—like a gift from the heavens or something. I didn't realize at first, didn't know anything special was about to happen, then *bam*! The teacher called Aya's name, and she answered. Her voice was as pretty as the rest of her—soft, melodious, and with a faintly British accent. I remembered those lilting vowels from when I was a kid. I'd tried, for days after meeting her, to emulate her posh string of words. I'd never managed to do so, but that hadn't stopped me from attempting, much to my parents' amusement.

I turned my head and caught her looking at me, a small smile on her face. She mouthed, "*Surprise!*" and then turned back to face the front.

I continued to stare, unable to tear my gaze away from the girl sitting the next row over and two seats up.

Aya was even prettier than I'd expected her to be. Her long, long hair was streaked with reddish highlights that added an interesting depth to the dark strands. Her nose was littered with freckles and the faint peeling of an old sunburn. Her chin was as stubborn and delicate as I'd remembered from our brief encounter all those years ago. Her eyes were even brighter, even more amazing up close than any gem my mom or grandmother had ever worn. Aya's cheekbones sat high in her thin face, her neck slender and elegant, and her body that slim, lithe shape most of the Hollywood elite spent thousands to try to create.

I sucked in a breath as I took her in. She shifted in her seat, giving me a partial view of her chest. She had *fabulous* tits: high and perky and definitely enough to fill my hand. I might have emitted a strangled breath as I stared at them. She glanced back, caught my gaze, and frowned.

My face burned, and I looked away. When I turned back, I caught her looking at me from under her lashes. That time, our gaze held until the bell rang. I couldn't remember what the teacher said, nor did I care.

My embarrassment dissipated as my excitement to actually speak to Aya grew. I leaped from my chair and wrapped her in a hug, letting my nose fall against the side of her neck. Aya felt so right, so *perfect* in my arms. Her hair smelled like fresh air and sunshine, the first of which was in short supply even in outdoorsy Austin. Too many cars had led to a layer of smog that I doubted Aya had seen in Nepal.

"I wasn't expecting you," I said, not caring that the voices around me rose in excited chatter. Nash Porter wasn't affectionate. Nash Porter didn't have girlfriends.

Aya hesitated. She sucked her plump, pink lower lip deep into her mouth.

Now, seeing it in person, I really wanted that lip in *my* mouth. I wanted that mouth on mine. And…shit. I breathed through the excitement and need even as I moved back enough that she wouldn't realize my body was jumping at her nearness.

"My grandfather's sick," she murmured.

Instant boner killer, and not at all the way I wanted to get there. I grabbed Aya's backpack and then my own. "Oh. Like sick or…*sick*?"

She hesitated, a frown tugging at her brows. "He's going to die soon. We're staying with him."

I winced even as I took her hand and led her out into the hall. "That totally sucks."

She nodded as her lashes dropped to her cheeks. Even sad, she was gorgeous.

I cleared my throat, hoping my body wouldn't betray me yet again. "That's a bad thing? Staying with your grandpa?"

"It's…unexpected."

That I could understand.

"I'd not met him until a few years ago when my parents divorced. I guess Mum's marriage caused a bitter rift between them. He told me last night he'd disinherited her until she came to her senses and kicked the rounder to the curb."

I smirked. "Rounder," I muttered. "Good British insult."

Every set of teenaged eyes in the hallway stared as we walked together, their gazes landing on our joined hands.

"Um…why are people staring at me?" Aya whispered, inching closer.

Nice. I liked her there, pressed into my side. I could feel the warmth of her skin against mine. I thought back to the day we'd met, how her hand had felt in mine as I pulled her out of the water.

Something had clicked then, and I felt a similar happiness now.

"They're not. They're staring at *me*. I don't hold hands. I don't really like the girls around here all that much."

"Nash!" She tried to extricate her fingers, but I gripped her hand even tighter.

"You're different, Ay. Always have been."

"Because you know me so well from text messages," she said, her tone on the snarky side. But she relaxed, no longer tugging her hand away. A shiver ran the length of my spine at her acquiescence. And when she met my gaze? *Perfection.*

"We've known each other for *years*. Most of our lives."

She laughed. "You didn't know my name."

"Didn't need to. You knew mine." I winked.

"Sure did, Superstar."

At my hot look, she dropped her gaze and tucked some of that luscious hair behind her ear.

I nearly purred. Then I saw Hugh from the corner of my eye, his arm draped over Naomi and a knowing look on his stupid face. I straightened my shoulders and lifted my chin. My thing with Aya was nothing like Hugh's besotted relationship with Naomi. She bossed him around, which was part of why I refused to hang out with either of them. I dropped Aya's hand.

"What's your schedule?"

She sighed. "Science, then English."

My smile grew as she rattled off her schedule. "Same as mine. Oh, this is *perfect*."

This time I did purr. Her startled gaze searched my face, and I thought I saw the flare of desire burning in the depths of those pretty violet eyes.

"You can take Lindsay Herrington-Smythe's seat," I said, my lip curling. "I can't stand that girl."

"I'm not stealing someone's seat," Aya replied, her face haughty. "That wouldn't be kind."

"Lindsay keeps trying to grab my junk," I said. *Total lie.* Well, she had stared at my crotch often enough to make me self-conscious.

And my dislike of her was the truth. Something about her reminded me of Lord—in the worst possible way. She took genuine pleasure in hurting others' feelings. It was one thing to be aloof, untouchable—I had perfected that art early and used it to my advantage—but Lindsay was mean.

Aya took a protective step closer. "I'll sit next to you," she said. She seemed to struggle to meet my gaze, her pupils dilated.

I wanted to fist pump. *Yes.* Aya Aldringham wanted me, too.

Her tongue darted out, bathing that plump lower lip I'd obsessed over for years. I leaned in closer, mesmerized. Her lips parted, her breath flooding past that luscious pink perfection in a tumble of heat. Desire licked hard and hot up my middle.

Someone bumped my shoulder, breaking the spell. I blinked and stepped back.

Fuck.

Fuckity fuck.

Aya was my *friend.* My only real friend. No way I was messing with that—not even if I suddenly needed her taste like I needed air.

I cleared my throat, my smile weak. "Great."

What had I gotten myself into?

"Where did *she* come from?" Lindsay asked her friend as she passed Aya and me in the hall later that afternoon. Lindsay narrowed her dark brown eyes, and her thin, bright red lips smashed flat as she stared at me holding Aya's hand, though she never broke her stride.

"Is she English?" Aya asked, her chin lifted toward Lindsay.

"Yeah. She's from some suburb of London. Her dad's in IT. He came here and set up a thinktank or something. He's kind of a big deal in Austin circles."

"Weird. I didn't realize Austin was so…"

"Urbane?" I asked. "Cultured?"

"International," Aya replied, her tone dry.

"I have no idea," Lindsay's friend, Stef, said as they paused a little farther down the hall.

Lindsay popped her gum while trying to give us a filthy glare. I held Stef's gaze long enough for her to flush and look away, though Lindsay remained too bold and angry to bow under my stare. I'd been practicing the expression after watching Camden Grace use it on an overstepping journalist this past weekend.

"What's with that look?" Aya asked.

"Something I'm trying out," I murmured, refusing to be the first to break eye contact with Lindsay.

Stef tugged at Lindsay's arm, finally leading her away. The girls turned the corner, cutting off the staring contest. Aya heaved a huge sigh of relief.

"You weren't kidding about the mean-girl vibe," Aya said.

"Wait for it," I told her. "The boys are just as gossipy and mean."

Aya leaned her head back and groaned. Somehow, I palmed her hip. Her warmth saturated my skin even through the denim. I flexed my fingers, enjoying the supple give of her flesh.

Aya's tits rose and fell as she glanced over my shoulder. Her voice came out a bit higher than normal, and her pulse pounded in her neck.

Already I craved her. How had I gone so long without this? How could I manage a full day, let alone *weeks* of being near her, needing to be nearer? Emotions jangled through me, terrifying in their ferocity.

Her lids lowered, her lashes covering her eyes. "Nash..."

"Omigod, Nash *likes* her," a girl squealed.

We both startled. I stepped back.

"This situation is scarier than those cliffs I showed you," Aya murmured.

"More dangerous, too," I deadpanned. "But don't worry, as long as you stick with me, kid, you're golden."

"Because of your parents?" Aya asked. Her wide eyes caught mine. "Do you think that's right? Fair?"

I shook my head. "Neither. But it's the pecking order. And it's not just my parents—my mom's father owns the hotels these people stay at all over the world. We're rich fuckers who lunch with global leaders. That's also why no one cares if I'm feeling sad or lonely or whatever."

"That's impossibly sad." Aya looked down.

"Maybe. But as much as they want to take me down—and they do, *so* bad—they can't touch me without pissing off the head of the RNC, DNC, SBU, Jetsetter Records, you name it."

"You never told me how you ended up in Austin," she said, tilting her head so all that glorious hair spilled down her neck, cascading over her chest. I nearly groaned. Being near Aya was the most perfect torture.

I shrugged and attempted a nonchalance I didn't feel. "My Pop Syad—my grandfather—he owns a large IT firm in addition to his hotels. He moved my mother here when she was a teenager, and she liked it. My dad bummed through all the live music venues. That's how they met. His band, Quantum, played lots of clubs and scored its first national record contract about ten years ago."

I frowned, my high of spending time with Aya fading as the realities of my life slammed back into me. For a few moments, Aya had managed to keep those worries at bay. Even after all this time, I didn't have much ability to create new music. The last song I'd composed had been another one with Cam, and Dad wasn't going to be happy when he found out about that.

Aya snorted. "The inability to touch you must drive these kids crazy."

I lifted my chin, trying not to think about how I wanted *her* to touch me—or where. "Lord the most. That guy *hates* me."

As if he knew I was talking about him, Lord lumbered over and bumped my shoulder hard, forcing me closer to Aya.

"Looks like Nashville's got himself a girlfriend. I wonder if she knows he used to cry about his mommy's drug problem."

I feigned a disappointed sigh, even as the bite of shame slid up the back of my neck. I had cried the year Lev died—blubbered in the bathroom—because it was the first time I'd had to sit at a lunch table without him.

"She likes vodka, dipshit. Coke was *so* last year. Might want to pass that on since your mom's known for her coke nose. Oh, right! You don't see her or her nose because your parents refuse to live in the same state as you."

Lord raised his fist, his face florid, but Aya stuck out her foot, tripping him as he hurtled toward me.

"How clumsy of you," she said, batting her long eyelashes. "Would you like a hand up?"

Aya started to bend down just as Lord rose with a snarl, slamming his shoulder into her chest. The impact caused her to fly backward into Hugh, who'd been walking by. He dropped his book bag and a big, messy pile of papers flew from his binder as he attempted to catch her. The two of them tumbled to the floor, Aya sprawled atop a befuddled Hugh.

Lindsay and Stef shrieked with laughter, sounding like hyenas ready to close in on their kill. They must have been lurking right around the corner. They were probably the ones who sent Lord to bug me. I never underestimated Lindsay's mean streak, and this situation seemed to be the kind both she and Lord lived for.

Hugh shifted, his hand sliding over Aya's chest. I heard a deep whooshing in my ears as her eyes widened and her jaw trembled.

"That's *it*," I said, my voice quiet but carrying an intensity that caused everyone in the hallway to stop.

I stepped closer and helped Aya up, even as red tinged the edges of my vision.

"You okay?" I asked, searching her face, desperate for reassurance.

She nodded, eyes wide, cheeks redder than the Oscar carpet.

"Yeah?" Lord said. He cracked his knuckles. "*That's it?* What the fuck does that even mean? You think you're going to take me down? By yourself." He snorted.

"I don't need to hit you, as enjoyable as that would be. I have much more effective means of dealing with your assholery."

Still, I pulled my arm back and shot my fist into Lord's Adam's apple. He gasped for air.

"Don't fuck with me, Lord. Don't touch my friends. You hear me?"

Lord choked, his face mottled but filled with hatred.

I wasn't done. I sent Steve a text. *Got a situation in the hallway. Lord Prescott threatened me and shoved my friends around. I want to hit him.*

I left off the *again* because Steve was going to be pissed when he found out I'd hit Lord in the first place.

My phone rang. "I'm on my way inside," Steve said. "And I'll take care of Lord."

"I want him gone, Steve," I snapped. "As in expelled. He shoved a girl."

I risked a look back at Aya, who I'd kept behind me, not willing to let Lord hurt her again. A flush burned under her tanned skin, and I liked the look on her. She was slightly exotic but completely familiar—an electric combination.

"I'll deal with Prescott," Steve said again.

Lord must have heard Steve's comment, because his mouth fell open and his eyes bugged. I didn't bother to hold back my smile. "*One phone call,*" I'd told Lord. I'd told them all. But until the douche monkey came at Aya, I hadn't cared enough to follow through.

That all changed when Lord put his hands on my girl.

My girl.

I gripped my phone tighter, needing it to tether me to the now. Shock and something warm settled in the angry swamp of my belly. For some reason, I didn't hate the thought of Aya being my girl as much as I probably should've.

Aya bent down now, along with Naomi and Hugh, to collect the papers strewn across the hallway. Hugh, the asshole that he was, stared down Aya's V-neck shirt, his mouth gaping like a freaking fish out of water, until Naomi elbowed him hard, right in the thigh.

I smirked, deciding I might actually like Naomi after all.

Lord stood up, his stance menacing. He raised his fists and launched himself at me. I managed to duck the first attempt—a right hook, but his left fist caught me in the ribs. I grunted. Over Lord's shoulder I caught a glimpse of two armed security guards running toward us, followed by the head of school and Steve.

"Get the Prescott shit off him now," Steve snapped to the guards. "Or I'll do it. And I won't be nice."

The guards each gripped one of Lord's arms, dragging him backward. Steve cast the bully a furious look.

"You okay?" he asked me.

I nodded, refusing to wince. But, holy hell, my ribs smarted. Lord had put a lot of effort into that punch.

"We'll need you to come to my office, Nash," the head of school said, a harried expression on his face.

"Sure."

Steve gave me a long look, his gaze landing on Aya, who was still helping collect papers. He frowned and gave me a nod. He laid his hand on my shoulder and squeezed. "Proud of you."

Well, he'd be less proud when he found out I'd nailed Lord in the throat, but whatever. Aya was safe.

"Give me a minute," I said.

Steve nodded, his gaze flashing back to Aya before he steered the head of school back down the hallway after a much-subdued Lord.

Aya rose and grabbed her bag from my arm.

"I'm heading to the loo," she said.

"You okay?" I asked her. "Your butt—"

"Is fine," she said. She glanced around at the dispersing crowd. "That was way too much excitement for my first day."

"Meet me at the school office," I said. I looked behind her at Hugh. He'd done his best to protect Aya, so I'd give him another chance. "You, too."

He fell into step beside me as Aya trotted off toward the bathroom.

"You stay away from her," I grunted as soon as Aya was out of earshot.

Hugh blinked to focus on me. "She invited me to sit with her at lunch," he said. "Me and Naomi—you know, my *girlfriend*."

"I don't want you near Aya," I said. "And do not look down her shirt again, you skeez."

"That just…they were right…" He cleared his throat. "I love Naomi. But Aya is nice, both in personality and to look at."

"That's the problem. She's new and she's nice, and I…"

I stopped. *Never, never admit when you want something, Nash.* That was my mother's best advice. Or at least the mantra she liked to drape over me. *If you do, people will use it as leverage, use it against you.*

"You what?" Hugh asked.

"That's why I invited her to sit with me," I muttered, avoiding his eyes. I'd nearly broken the rule for *a girl.*

"Well, I guess I'll see you and Aya at your table."

Hugh entered the office while I gritted my teeth, cupping my aching side. Suddenly nothing was going right today. I yanked the door wide and stomped inside.

Steve and the staff assumed my bad attitude was because of the fight Lord started, and I didn't bother to correct them. Nor did I register Lord's dismissal from Holyoke. From what I remembered, in a vague, underwater-type of way, Lord never said anything. The punk just disappeared from the school, whisked away like the filth he was. Instead, I focused on listing all the reasons I couldn't give in to the attraction between Aya and me. Why I didn't want it.

Then she walked into the headmaster's office, and the tension drained from my muscles and my head.

I was so totally fucked.

As we walked back to class, late, I asked Aya to sit with me at lunch. She blushed and dropped her eyes.

"I said I'd sit with Hugh since he tried to keep me from hitting the floor when the 'Prescott shit' started causing problems."

I smiled. Her imitation of Steve was spot on.

"Plus," Aya said, no longer meeting my gaze, "I thought maybe we could hit pause."

"Why?" I stopped walking and leaned against a row of blue lockers. She wanted to talk, so we'd talk.

She stared down at the ends of her hair, as if mesmerized by them. "I'm not sure about what you did back there…to Lord. Was that necessary?"

"*So* necessary," I said on a sigh.

She looked up and met my gaze.

"And long overdue." I waved my hand. "Everyone is going to be happy about Lord leaving. Except maybe Lindsay."

She glanced around, but no one was out here in the hallway. Her shoulders slowly relaxed. "Well, I'm still sitting with Hugh and Naomi. I *promised*."

That seemed to be the end of the conversation, though I still wanted to argue. Aya must have seen the gleam in my eye because she narrowed hers and put her hands on her hips.

"I *promised*, Nash."

She turned and marched down the hall. I caught up to her and grabbed her hand, leading her back to the right door. She muttered *thanks* but seemed unwilling to meet my gaze.

Whatever.

I settled into my normal seat, scowling when I noted Aya was across the room. That wouldn't fly. But I'd fix the seating situation tomorrow. I listened with half an ear while the teacher talked about the STEM interdisciplinary project we'd be working on for the rest of the semester. Instead of finals, half the teachers planned to use the project as a large chunk of our grade.

I noted that Aya perked up, her eyes alight with interest.

Right. She loved math and science. Her goal was acceptance at a top-tier engineering school. I had no doubt she'd achieve it… and leave me behind.

I settled back in my desk, arms crossed, and spaced out.

A new melody drifted through my head, and I opened my notebook, writing down the notes, then the lyrics.

The snippet was angsty—perfect for a country tune or an indie rock ballad, depending on which direction I went with the strings. Banjo would be more bluegrass or country…but cello—yes! The deep, melancholy thrum of a cello overlaid with two different guitars. I scribbled the notes through the bell, ignoring everyone in the room.

I finally stood, stretched, winced, and noted Aya hovering near the door.

She was as drawn to me as I was to her.

"He hit you hard," she said. "Do you need a doctor?"

I shook my head as I packed my backpack. Since we'd missed one class and entered this one late, it was now lunchtime.

I considered switching tables and refusing to sit with Aya. I wasn't sure I liked her exerting power over me. Not sure at all. But I wasn't willing to let her out of my sight, which meant…

"Let's go eat," I muttered.

Chapter 9
Nash

I met Aya's mother and grandfather that afternoon when she invited me back to her house after school. I rather liked them both, and since then we'd been hanging out at her place after school every day. We'd settled into a nice routine. Yesterday, I'd spent an hour or so with her mother while Aya used power tools in the workshop near the garage. The noise gave me a headache, so I'd begged off. Mrs. Didri-Aldringham made me a cup of chai and offered me a couple of Madeleines—as if I'd pass on cookies.

That's what Aya's mom went by—Didri-Aldringham—a hyphenated version of her life. "*Bifurcated by divorce*," she'd told me. "*I refuse to give up my daughter's last name to please my ex-husband.*" Her dark eyes had sparkled with mischief as she munched her cookie. "*He can deal.*"

Yeah, I liked Ay's mom a lot. And Mr. Didri was cool, too. He sat in his lush garden and smoked some weird tobacco. His wild stories were way more fun than sitting at home, waiting for Aya to text or Cam to call. So, I spent more and more of my time at the Didri mansion, enjoying their close-knit family.

It wasn't like my own parents cared. My mom hopped a plane after embarrassing herself in front of Aya and me, and my dad finally showed up yesterday to offer me the chance to perform the song I'd written over the past few days—a tune he'd found in my room. One I hadn't planned to share with him. He said if I let him record it, playing with him on tour could be my birthday present.

That meant my gift would be months late and only if I let him use the song on his album. Some deal. I'd considered talking to Cam about that, but I wanted to perform. The itch had grown, but I needed my own material to create an album. *Or* I needed recognition for the songs I'd already written, which made Dad's offer perfect, since I still seemed to have a barely functioning muse.

Hugh and Naomi were excited when I told them and Aya the next day at lunch. They'd joined Aya and me every day for over two weeks now. Honestly, I was kind of over spending time with them.

"I promised," Aya said when I brought up the lunch arrangement on our walk home from school. "We've been doing it for weeks now. What's the big deal?"

Part of the reason I'd waited this long was because I liked Hugh. His wicked sense of humor made me smile, and I hadn't done much of that since Lev died. And even though we'd had that falling out freshman year, he'd invited me to his parties and stood next to me when Lord had been a dick. Hugh had been a friend to me even when I'd refused to reciprocate. So, yeah, I liked this new arrangement better.

But I *didn't* like sharing Aya's attention. Besides school, she spent a few hours each day on her STEM project, which did allow me to jot down more bits of music. But still…we were busy. And I didn't want to share her, especially not with my father's tour coming so soon.

I narrowed my eyes at Aya. "You promised," I said, my tone dry.

"Yes, Nash. And when you promise, you have to follow through."

I should have known. Aya treated promises like sacred objects. Clearly, she wasn't from the same culture as me. If she were, she'd understand promises were empty, made to be crumpled, trampled, kicked out of the way the moment they became inconvenient. Not unlike me.

I shut that thought down quick. So what if my parents weren't around? I had Steve at home. I had friends in Cam and Ay.

"Fine," I conceded to Aya's lunch negotiation. "But you have to admit Hugh can be obnoxious."

Aya hesitated. "He's not, really. He's nervous around you. He told me how you quit hanging out with him because of Naomi."

I crossed my arms over my chest. "Good. He deserved it."

"Oh, come on, Nash. Give the guy a chance. He loves her."

I growled in frustration as I walked on, ignoring Steve, who inched forward on the street next to us in some fancy-fuck car I couldn't care less about. Yeah, most kids would give anything to live my life, but I'd rather have my parents around. My dad hadn't been home in a week, and I was starting to feel…

I wasn't sure.

Scared, maybe. Like I had when I'd seen Aya wading into the water that day when we were little. A feeling of inevitability had caused me to pay closer attention to the situation. My mom had been absent off and on for years now, thanks to her career. And, sure, my dad screwed around, but since Lev died, I'd realized I felt…I felt more and more like my family didn't care what happened to me.

Like I didn't matter.

That was a difficult pill to swallow—one that hurt an awful lot as it slid down into my churning gut.

"What?" Aya raised her gaze to mine, and I stumbled over my feet.

Those eyes were liquid violets. And her skin glowed angel-soft, smoother than velvet. I'd do just about anything for her—even walk in this heat like she'd asked me to. Sit with Hugh. Fuck. Be buddies with Hugh. Whatever. I just…I needed Aya to be happy.

Admitting I wanted her happy was easier than admitting I needed her. Wanted her, hell to the yes.

"N-nothing," I stammered. No way I could tell her what I was thinking. She could hurt me with those secrets. But I *wanted* to tell her. I wanted to so badly I could taste the words on my tongue.

Aya's long hair pressed against her neck before shifting to tumble down her arm. She had thirteen freckles on her nose. I knew because I'd counted them. Every day.

"My grandfather went to see a specialist yesterday," Aya said. "The one in Houston."

"Oh?"

Aya hadn't mentioned his illness since the first day, and I hadn't pushed.

She dropped her gaze to the ground. "He's down to weeks, he said." Aya swallowed what sounded like an entire ball of yarn. "Yeah. His cancer metastasized."

"Shit, Ay. That's…" I fisted my hands as rage and…something else…something I couldn't identify…swept over me, creating a tidal wave of anger. "How's your mom holding up?"

"She's a bit of a mess. I think she expected to have more time with Jeddi."

Aya called Mr. Didri *Jeddi*. It meant grandpa in Arabic, which, like French, Aya spoke well.

"Why Jeddi and not Grandpère?" I asked.

"I'm not sure, but if I had to guess, it's because his connection to Tunisia made him different. Jeddi likes to stand out."

I smiled at that, totally getting the dude's thinking.

"He really doesn't like my dad. I think that's because he and my mum are fighting a lot. Last time I talked to Dad, he told me I'd need proper schooling if I ever wanted to be accepted in the peerage." Aya cleared her throat, keeping her gaze forward. "I told him I was going to get my degree in aeronautical engineering and work at the JPL. He doesn't think I'm smart enough."

I frowned. "That's…weird. Who gives a crap about a bunch of wigged-up old dudes, anyway?"

Aya laughed, but it sounded bitter, like she was all edges inside and trying not to be cut by them.

"My father. He married my mother because she was so rich. He didn't understand the depth of the British obsession with their own—and how much of an outsider my mum would always remain. Americans aren't impressed much by titles. Wealth wins the day here, and my grandfather has *that* in spades."

"He told me he and my Pop Syad used to hang out, were even business partners for a while. And I bet they were hellraisers in their day."

"I bet you're right." We walked in silence but from the corner of my eye, I saw Aya searching my face. "What were you thinking about in the hall? That day you fought with Lord?"

I blew out a breath before I answered her with a partial truth. "My brother."

She blinked at me. "Lev," she murmured.

I wasn't surprised she remembered. Aya was like that—able to remember all the important details I shared, and many of the unimportant ones, too.

"Was he younger or older?" she asked.

I shoved my hands into my pockets, justifying my telling her because everyone else already knew the sordid truth.

"He was a year and a half older." I blinked back the burning sensation.

"What happened?" she asked, tears already swimming in her eyes.

"He died." The words, even though years had passed now, hurt to speak.

"I know that. How?"

I continued to walk, my Chucks pattering across the straight, perfect sidewalk. I'd never told the whole story, never shared the details with anyone. Never intended to.

"My parents were fighting." The words tumbled from my mouth, desperate to break free from the prison I'd shoved them into as soon as I realized Lev wasn't going to wake up.

"You don't have to tell me," Aya said, her voice soft.

I felt her palm slip into place against mine, felt her fingers squeeze.

"I've never told anyone," I said.

Her eyes held patience and understanding. "I kind of figured that."

I turned and stared straight ahead, trying not to enjoy the feel of Aya's hand in mine, the warmth of her body radiating against my arm. I tried to ignore the soft brush of her hair, the sweet scent that emanated from her body.

I failed.

I inhaled hard. Did I want to talk about this?

No way.

Was I going to?

Apparently.

"My brother caught my dad with a groupie—at our house. That was the beginning of the end of their relationship. When Lev's anger started spiraling…he was a mess. Anyway, Mom put Lev in therapy. And I guess the therapist told her about Dad having sex with women in our house."

Aya leaned in closer. Her luscious tit pressed against my biceps. That felt good. She felt good. Perfect, really. That's what allowed me to continue.

"Your mother is a beautiful woman. What more could your father want?"

I shrugged, immediately regretting the action because it bumped Aya's soft flesh away from me.

"I don't know. Mom used to be so fun, so present, but even before Lev died, when he was so angry and acting out, everything just kind of fell apart. Now? She's…empty. And a drunk—high most of the time. Maybe Dad wants a woman who can have an actual conversation, not just an ornament."

Aya made a squeaky noise but managed to keep her mouth shut.

My father knew the Carolina of my youth was gone. Maybe he had known it for years and just didn't care. Or—and this worried me more—Dad cared too much to sever the link, which was why they kept spiraling back into alcoholism and loud fights and the pain of losing Lev.

"We'd just come back from touring with my dad. Lev wanted to get out of the house, get away from their constant fighting. He said he'd heard them—it had something to do with us." *With me.*

But I swallowed that back, unwilling to share that piece of information. I worried it was why my mom had become so emotionally distant and my dad refused to be near me. I hated where those thoughts led, to the place where it was my fault Lev was dead, that my family was broken.

"Lev..." I bit the inside of my cheek. No one knew this part of the story. Not my parents. Not the police. Definitely not the press.

She laid her hand on my chest, right over my pounding heart. "Whatever you tell me, Nash, will always be between us. Just us. I promise."

I inhaled. Aya promised.

Just us.

Lev used to say that, but in a different context. "It's just us, brother. Porters against the world." And we'd fist bump.

I should have hugged Lev more. I should have told him how much he meant to me.

"He took a bunch of my mom's pills," I said, the words rushing out, tumbling over each other, like the waves at the beach. "Or maybe my dad's. I don't know. He was really out of it." I huffed.

"He did it in front of them, but they didn't notice—they just kept fighting. Mom knocked the phone from Dad's hand. It ended up..."

Next to Lev.

That's when shit really went south.

"Lev grabbed it and made a beeline for the dock. I thought he'd throw the phone in the lake."

I didn't have to tell Aya that I lived right on the water—that was the best address, the most expensive piece of real estate in an overpriced market. And the Syads and the Porters had the best of everything. Plus, she'd been there.

"My dad ran after him, telling Lev to give him back his phone."

My father had been texting another woman. A woman he never met because of Lev's death. In that, Lev got his wish.

"Lev yelled *no*, that he wouldn't give back the phone and our dad should actually listen to our mom. That he should stop banging random chicks. Dad was too slow. *I* was too slow."

I swallowed.

"Lev jumped out into the water. We weren't supposed to do that, not at night, but he couldn't have been thinking straight. He was so fucking high." I gulped. "He must have tripped. He just..."

Aya wrapped her free arm around my biceps, tugging my whole arm against her pillowy chest. Reliving that night was the deepest hell, one I typically refused to acknowledge.

Maybe that's why it took me a full minute to realize I was crying. Aya dropped my arm and pulled me into her embrace. I pressed my nose against the juncture of her shoulder and neck. I sobbed and blubbered and shook as the loss of Lev rolled over me, pulling me under, not unlike the lake that later spat my brother's limp, broken body onto the shore.

"He was my best friend," I gasped, my entire body shuddering.

And that was the real reason I'd kept Hugh at arm's length. He wasn't Lev. Neither was Aya. No one could replace my big brother.

Aya said nothing. She held me, rocking as my sobs grew in intensity. Once I calmed some, she said, "That's why you were so worried about me—all those years ago. You'd been taught to be careful in the water."

"Always."

She nodded, and I liked the feel of her silk hair shifting against my skin.

"Are you ready to finish it?"

I licked my lips, tasting the wetness of my tears—or maybe remembering the water on my face.

"Our neighbor heard the yelling, I guess. He came out, he called the cops, he pulled me out of the water before…before…"

Before I drowned, too. Because I wouldn't have stopped searching.

"He's the guy you talk to?"

"Yeah. Cam. Camden Grace."

She hummed deep in her chest. "Tell him thank you for me—thank you for saving your life."

"He did, didn't he?" I muttered. "I hadn't realized. I should thank him myself."

Aya nuzzled her nose against my cheek. "I bet he doesn't want it," she whispered into my ear. "I bet he's glad you're here, and that's enough for him. I know that's how I'd feel in his position."

Eventually, I pulled back, my eyes downcast, embarrassment swirling through me.

Part of me wanted to dive into the fancy car idling at the curb. Part of me wanted to lash out at Aya for making me talk about Lev, for making me remember and *feel*.

But instead Aya cupped my cheek, lifted up on her tiptoes, and kissed me. It was a soft, simple brush of her lips across mine.

This touch of lips seemed to say: *I see your grief, and I want to make it better. You mean something to me. You are special.*

I let my mouth respond: *You mean something to me, too. You see me, and you being here with me makes my life better.*

The kiss was perfect. Like Aya.

Just what I needed.

We stood, mouths meshed, tasting each other in small sips as our bodies inched closer. When I started to shift, planning to deepen the kiss, she cupped my cheeks. I wrapped my arms around her waist and pulled her flush against me. We held on, eyes closed, lips touching, blending under the dubious shade of the live oaks. Finally, Aya shifted, gasping for breath. Her eyes were wide and full of emotion.

We stared at each other until she gripped my shirt and pressed her nose into my pec. I tightened my hold, never wanting to let her go.

Chapter 10
Aya

My grandfather wobbled on through the sultry month of May. "*Holding on tight*," he said, to have more time with me.

I loved spending time with him, even as I worried about my mother's health. My entire life seemed to be veering off in a direction that would alter me substantially.

Nash understood because his parents' relationship was more messed up each day. They seemed to be communicating by one-upping each other with parties and alcohol, always seen in the company of a beautiful person who wasn't their spouse—and rarely in Austin.

In fact, neither of his parents had been home in weeks. The tension between them skyrocketed when Brad once again tried to fire Steve. This time, it was Nash's mom who refused Brad's request.

Neither Nash nor I knew what to make of that mess, and Carolina hadn't wanted to talk about Steve when Nash called her. I sat with him as he tried.

"*He seems to be taking care of you*," Carolina had said in response to Nash's question about Steve.

"*I guess. But I'd prefer you were around*," Nash told her.

She sighed. "*It's just so hard, Nash, being there right now*."

I wanted to ask her if she'd considered her son, but I managed to bite my tongue.

Nash hated the media and his mother's tearful reasons for staying away, but there wasn't much he could do. He deflected comments at school like a pro, and I tried hard to make sure few people bothered him, just like Hugh did. While I wouldn't call the guys close, Nash had thawed toward Hugh and included him in some of our weekend activities.

Not tonight, though. Tonight, Nash and I were outside on the deck behind my house. The temperature was dropping, and I shivered a little, but I wasn't going to suggest we head inside. I liked the sound of the lake lapping against the dock below and the soft strum of Nash's fingers over the strings of his guitar. He'd grown taller again, and his light brown hair was shaggier, hanging in his eyes and down the back of his neck, much to Steve's clear annoyance. Darkness descended slowly as the sun finished setting, the last faint hints of red dissipating over the water, leaving it a thick, opaque void. I shivered and refocused on Nash.

He lay on his back in one of the teakwood loungers while I lay on my side in the one next to his, watching him play. The white cushions were thick and downy, and I snuggled deeper as I ran my fingertip over my malas.

Nash stared up into the sky as he strummed idly, humming a tune. I liked watching him step more and more out of his shell. I loved that here with me, he was just Nash.

"My mom's upset that I'm going to tour with my dad," he said.

I wasn't surprised, just as I wasn't surprised that Carolina had chosen to stay in Europe instead of returning to visit her son. I'd read on a French gossip site that she was actually in a rehabilitation center—very discreet—and this wasn't the first time. I'd considered telling Nash, but I didn't want to stress him out more.

"Are you going to miss me?" he asked, glancing over.

More than you can imagine. "Yes."

"Then come with me."

"I can't. I'm attending the summer program at MIT."

"C'mon, Ay. You have plenty of time for school shit during the school year."

"Actually, I don't. And this will help me get into a top-tier college."

He turned toward me, his pouty face adorable. "The tour won't be as much fun without you. I really want you there."

I did, too. I wanted to be with Nash more than anything. But if I didn't get into MIT or Stanford, or even UT's Cockrell School of Engineering, my dad would lean hard on my mother, trying to force me into a British university. I couldn't understand why he'd taken an interest in my life. But since we'd moved back to Austin, he'd been making more and more noise about me moving to England.

Reginald Aldringham had managed to finagle a viscount title from his current wife's family, which made him an actual peer of the realm. Not that we discussed such things. Our typical conversations were barely more than a perfunctory greeting, an assurance that my mother was still alive, and then a litany of his "plans" for my future. He didn't seem to get that I didn't want to see him, let alone live with him, which made this summer program all the more important. Only a few students were accepted, and it would set me apart from the many others who would apply for the same limited college spots.

My burgeoning mood began to sour. Ever since that time he'd kissed me, Nash had kept me at arm's length, always reminding me we were friends. I flopped onto my back and stared up at the sky, angry tears burning the backs of my eyes.

"Why are you mad?" he asked, setting the guitar aside.

"Who says I'm mad?" I sounded angry.

I gritted my teeth. No matter what I said, he would find a way to circumvent my denials. This was the problem with spending so much time together, but I couldn't stop.

He slid onto the cushion next to me, aligning his lanky frame to mine. He positioned himself with his cheek cradled on his palm as he stared down at me. He wore an orange T-shirt with the name of some band on it—most of Nash's shirts were from bands he'd met on one of his dad's tours.

I liked that about him. I liked *everything* about him. I was pretty sure I loved him, actually. Gazing up into his brown eyes, so filled with past grief and hope, made me ache. I clenched my fists to keep from reaching for him, desperate to tug him down to me, to kiss him again.

I looked away. "You don't want a science nerd on a rock tour. I'd just be in the way."

He gripped my chin, forcing my gaze back to his. My chest warmed and something soft, special spread through it.

"You are *not* a nerd. *You* are a math whiz, and you won that engineering award at school when you'd only been there for a few weeks. Most of the rest of the kids had prepped for their projects all year, Ay. That's smart *and* badass. And it's more than enough to get you into the school of your choice. You don't need this extra program."

My face flushed with pleasure, making me thankful for the darkness. "I don't know…"

He flopped forward, pressing his forehead to my neck. "*Come on*. Live a little."

Then he began to hum again. I knew this tune. It was one he hummed often: "Something" by George Harrison, he'd told me.

I softened against him as he began to sing the words. He had a beautiful voice—deep and rich, like dark chocolate.

We lay out there for another hour before he began to pester me again. I turned and flicked his nose. "Ugh. Stop it."

"Once you say yes."

I raised my eyebrows. "I'll think about it."

He smirked as he hugged me closer. "That basically means yes."

My chest was smashed to his, and my nipples definitely took note. So did my lady parts. Before I could lift my thigh over his, Nash started, seeming to realize how close we were.

He rolled off the lounger and picked up his guitar. "Want to hear what I've been working on?"

I wanted to weep but instead I nodded. "Sure."

He played a beautiful tune. I closed my eyes and pretended the girl the boy was in love with was me.

Jeddi died in his sleep at the end of June, just a couple of days before Nash had planned to head out on tour with his father. Instead he postponed his trip to hang out at my house. I remained listless no matter how much he tried to cheer me up. Yes, part of the issue was my grandfather's death, but most of my worry stemmed from the fear that Nash would find a girlfriend—or simply hook up with multiple girls throughout the tour. Of course, I couldn't tell him that, and he didn't push me, even when my mother bought my ticket to Boston for the program at MIT.

The day before the funeral, Steve and my mother chatted in the kitchen while Nash and I drifted down toward the covered dock on the lake.

"What's wrong?" His lovely brown eyes beseeched me. "Can I help?"

I bit my lip, unsure how to bring up my fears.

"You're gorgeous and talented. I'm sure you won't lack for company," I managed to choke out. My head ached from keeping tears at bay. But I wouldn't cry for the end of my time with Nash—that seemed to cheapen my grief over my grandfather's death.

Nash stopped swinging his feet above the water. I kept my gaze outward, thankful for my sunglasses.

"Is *that* why you don't want to come on tour?"

I squinted, trying to make out whether the bird in the distance was a pelican or an egret. The sun's glare off the water made my eyes water, further blurring my vision. That was my story, anyway.

"You're the one who sent me pictures of the last tour," I finally said. "I told you, I'm a book nerd—"

He grabbed my hand. "You're my best friend. You're smart and funny and—"

"I don't belong on a rock tour," I said, shaking off his hand. "I'm going inside."

"Aya…" Nash trailed off, but I kept walking.

The next day, I wept at Jeddi's funeral, and my mum held one of my hands while Nash sat on my other side, stone-faced, holding the other. Much as I'd planned to push him away, I found myself burrowing tighter against him after I said my final goodbye.

"That sucked," he said after the service, tugging his tie loose as he flopped back on my bed.

We'd retreated to my bedroom, but we could hear the murmur of the crowd downstairs. Many had come to pay their respects to Irwan Didri, medical engineering pioneer and self-made billionaire. This was my last night with Nash, and I didn't want to miss any of it.

I kicked off my heels and set them in my closet while Nash sprawled horizontally across my bed, staring up at the high ceiling. He looked at home against the ruched comforter and pile of pillows. Perfect really.

And he was leaving me.

"Holding my hand was terrible for you?" I asked, attempting a joke. My tears threatened to fall, and I tried to turn away before Nash saw them.

He sat up on his elbow and tugged me close, tumbling me against him so he was once more lying on the bed, while I lay on his chest. He brushed the wetness from my cheeks. "No. Seeing you sad. Watching you grieve. I don't want you to do that again, Aya."

"This is life."

"I don't remember my dad's parents," he said into the thickening void.

"I'm sorry you don't have memories."

Nash sighed. "I'm not. Everyone says they were selfish. They were always coming to my dad with their hands out."

I squeezed his hand tighter in mine. "I don't have any grandparents left." I tried to smile. "It's not like I knew him all that long."

Nash shifted me to his side, his gaze intense as he studied my face. I lowered my eyes. Talking about feelings between us was a definite no-go for Nash. Sure, part of me was hurt by that, but I also understood. We'd both been through so much. Changing our relationship when we'd somehow become each other's emotional center seemed foolhardy.

That didn't stop me from yearning, though. And I did with *everything* inside me.

"When do you go to Boston?" Nash asked.

I tensed. "Next week."

"I'm going to miss you," he said. He let out a long sigh.

"It'll be like it was when I was in Nepal." It wouldn't. Our relationship had changed when we met in person. My attraction to him strengthened, but evidently Nash didn't return those feelings.

That's why I had to put distance between us. I couldn't let him do all that work. So that's why I had to reject his request for me to go on tour. I had my courses, my future in aeronautical engineering. I'd been fascinated by the topic for years and had taken apart many of the well pumps my mother's nonprofit had brought to villages. Mum had sighed and asked me to put them back together. Then she'd praised me for how well the wells drew water.

She loved me for what and who I was. Nash liked me, too, *as a friend*. Dread washed over me as I worried about the photos he'd soon send me—of him and his gorgeous girlfriend.

My stomach ached as we lay there, side by side.

"What are you worried about, really?" he asked. "I'll fix it."

My stomach erupted in butterflies. "You hooking up with girls," I blurted. I blushed so hard it felt as if my face had flash-burned.

His gaze turned solemn as he drew my hand to his chest. "I don't want to hook up with other girls."

I held my breath. Did that mean…?

"I've seen what sex does to relationships, Aya. It complicates things, hurts people. My dad bangs all those women, and now my mom won't even live in the same house."

His parents had legally separated the previous week, and Carolina was keeping a low profile in Europe. Nash said she was staying with Pop Syad and making noise for him to join her in Paris. Neither of us was looking forward to that further separation—and it was another reason he kept pushing me to join him on tour.

"Your father's a cheater," I snapped. "And you're not even in a relationship." *Much to my continued disappointment.* Well, as long as Nash chose me…but he hadn't.

He grunted.

I laid my hand on his chest. "I'm sorry. That wasn't helpful." I sighed. "I don't like you being sad either," I whispered.

"I'm not sad." He kept my hand cupped against his chest. "But I am going to miss you."

Damn Nash and his raspy, whispery plea that shot straight to my heart. I bit my lip. I couldn't tell him no.

I managed to keep my mouth shut, and exhaustion weighed on me, trying to drag me under.

"It's not how long you know someone," Nash murmured sometime later.

"What?" I asked.

"You said you hadn't known your grandfather for very long. But I don't think it's how long you know someone that matters."

His voice was so quiet, barely more than the shape of his lips. I rolled toward him, resting my hand on his chest. He played with my hair's ends before smoothing his hand down my head, cradling my nape. He pressed a kiss to my temple.

This was the side of Nash few experienced. The one that made me melt and yearn.

"It's how well the other person sees you. And I see you, Aya Jane Aldringham."

Chapter 11
Aya

I pressed my palms to my quivering belly. "I'm not sure I made the right choice," I whispered.

"What?" Nash asked.

I turned to smile at him, but it likely appeared more as a grimace. "Just nervous is all."

Nash rolled his eyes even as he took a protective step closer to me, which caused my pulse to ratchet upward. "Everything will be fine."

I nibbled my lip, needing to change the subject. "What's this room called?"

Nash shrugged. "The green room, I guess. Just a place for the band and some of the staff to hang out before and after the show."

"And no one will be upset we're here?" I asked, fidgeting.

"Stop worrying, Ay. It's all good. My dad'll come in soon now that they're done with the sound check."

But I couldn't shake the worry that plagued me. My skin itched as I waited for the angry call from my mother. I'd let her know I planned to travel with Nash this week—but she thought I'd still head up to Boston for my course after that.

Which I should. I would. I *definitely* would. Not just because of the cost—which was significant—but because the professors expected me. I just hadn't been able to resist Nash's sweetness last night, so here I was. This was the best of both worlds, really. I'd see what Nash was up to, and then go do what I needed to do.

Nash leaned against the wall next to me and began to hum. It wasn't loud enough for me to pick up the tune.

"What are you humming?" I asked.

He blinked, as if shocked I could hear him. "Nothing."

I raised an eyebrow, and he ducked his head, abashed. Tenderness welled up, and I pressed my hands harder against my stomach to keep from reaching for him.

"It sounded pretty," I said.

He shrugged, bumping my arm. *Shit.* I'd inched closer to him. I was always doing that—seeking out his warmth.

"It's just a bit of a song."

"One I've heard?"

I knew the answer to that before Nash shook his head. Suddenly he created music. No, that was the wrong word—he *composed* it. Over the past few weeks, music had seemed to pour out of him, and I was fascinated by his ability to hear not just different note and tones, but a variety of instruments.

"Well, Mr. Superstar, if you ever decide to write it down, I'd love to hear it," I said.

He snorted. "Mr. Superstar? It's a good thing you have that posh British accent, Ay, because the crap you spout is ridiculous."

I nudged him with my shoulder, ignoring the flutter in my chest as we touched. "You don't seem to mind it."

His smile softened, as did his eyes. "Nah. I don't mind. Hey, I'm glad your mom was so cool with you coming along."

My eyes prickled, and I swallowed hard. “She…ah…well… it wasn’t her favorite.”

Nash stilled. “What aren’t you telling me?” He whipped out his phone and started typing. “She better not hate me for having you here.”

“Unlikely, seeing as she seems to think you created and move the sun,” I said.

He preened, casting me a side-eye, those soft lips turning up in a smile. I forced my gaze away.

“She does, doesn’t she?” he asked.

I made a noncommittal sound, unwilling to share what my mother had said about Nash the first time I’d brought him home. I was still shocked by her response to him. Every time she saw him, she beamed as brightly as the aforementioned star, seeming to bask in his presence. Sure, Nash was good-looking… fine, he was *gorgeous*. Not just his facial structure, which was divine—but then, with Carolina Syad for a mom, it would be hard not to be beautiful. No, Nash’s body was also well-proportioned if a bit skinny. In the time I’d known him, he’d already begun to fill out, turning him into a devastating assault on women of all ages. Me, especially.

But he was also polite, solicitous, and poised—an unusual combination in teen boys. And when Nash felt comfortable, he was funny. Sure, he used sarcasm and dry wit to diffuse conversations and deflect unwanted attention, but there was a silliness to him that he rarely let people see. My mum and I saw it, often now.

“Hmm. Good. She said she’s not mad,” Nash said, beaming.

“She who?”

"Your mom."

I scowled, clenching my fists. "Omigod! Stop meddling in my life."

"No can do, pretty girl," he said, still on his phone.

That was good because he didn't see me biting my lip and trying hard not to smile. The nickname was silly, but I adored it.

"She said you better call her later, though, because you have some logistics to work through." He raised an eyebrow and looked at me. "I told her I'd make sure you did."

Nash could be so annoyingly responsible when he took the notion. Typically, he saved those moments for *my* life.

"I'll deal with my mum when I'm ready." And I wasn't ready. Seriously, what was I doing here? "When do we see this Camden Grace fellow you talk about?"

"Early next week. In Nashville."

"Great. I'll get to meet him, then." His lashes were as sun-kissed as the hair on his head. My gaze traced the sharp lines of his cheekbones.

"Why wouldn't you?" he asked. His eyes widened. "You're going to the thing at MIT. How long is this course anyway?"

"Six weeks."

He scowled. "Fuck, Ay. That's most of the summer."

I shrugged, pretending his disappointment didn't bother me. It shouldn't. *We aren't a couple.* He didn't want to be. "I'm still shocked I was accepted."

"You shouldn't be. I told you, you're really smart." He clenched his jaw. "I won't ask you to stay with me again. But I want to."

"Because your dad's been all weird?"

Nash shrugged. "I don't know what's up his ass. His album isn't doing as well as he'd hoped."

I nudged his shoulder. "Probably because you didn't write the songs."

He shot me a shy smile that made me a bit woozy. Once Nash realized his impact on me, I'd be totally screwed. "You think the last album was better?" he asked, his tone hopeful.

"Far superior," I said in a haughty tone, using my most precise British enunciation.

Nash chuckled. "Yeah, me too." His smile slipped. "Dad's not much of a songwriter."

"Why didn't he ask you to write any of the songs?"

Nash shrugged. "He did, but nothing was clicking for me. Then he holed up with Beanie back in February. Once they started, he never even invited me to the studio."

Nash wasn't a fan of Quantum's drummer. I hadn't met the guy yet, but from Nash's stories, he sounded condescending. And that was his best quality.

"That's okay. You said you've been hanging out with Cam, right? Didn't his last album go gold or something?"

Nash laughed. "Platinum. His first single broke the daily download record for a week straight."

"And you wouldn't have had anything to do with that song, would you?"

His blush was adorable. I wanted to press my cheek to his, have his embarrassment warm me.

"A little," he mumbled.

"Well, I can see who has the talent in the family," I teased.

Steve walked back into the room and Nash straightened away from me, eyeing his bodyguard.

"Nash, my boy!"

I turned to find a tall, lithe man—probably about twenty-five years older than Nash and me—striding forward, a huge smile on his face.

His blond hair appeared disheveled, as if someone had been running their fingers through it. His eyes twinkled with mischief, and the dimples in his cheeks hinted at a sweetness I was sure he used to his advantage with the ladies, which probably accounted for the crazy hair.

"Beanie," Nash said.

Nash pocketed his phone and fist bumped the other guy, who studied me like my father did—as if wondering if I had any worth. I blinked up at him, straightening my spine.

"Ay, this is Quantum's drummer, Beanie. Beanie, this is Aya."

"Welcome, Aya," Beanie said. His eyes remained cool, assessing, as they slid over my body. He turned back to Nash. "Your girlfriend?"

"Thanks," I said before Nash could respond. No need to tell the world he didn't find me attractive enough to date. "I've never been to a concert before," I added, feeling heat rush to my cheeks.

"Kinda hard when you've spent most of the past couple of years scaling the Himalayas," Nash said, turning toward me.

"The Himalayas, huh?" Beanie asked, eyebrows raised. He considered me for a long moment. "Sounds daring."

A small group of other people soon surrounded us, including Brad Porter, Nash's dad. He had a beer in his hand and a glint of anger in his eye.

"My mother runs a nonprofit, and we spent time there, helping the local tribes build wells and improve their medical care," I said.

"A veritable Mother Teresa," Beanie noted.

I licked my lips, the excitement I'd felt moments before fizzling. I blinked back tears. The very world seemed to weigh on my shoulders. Nash eased closer to me, his body angled forward as if ready to spring into action against any threat. "That's no way to talk to my friend."

I reached out, my fingers wrapping around his wrist, tugging him backward.

Steve stepped forward, his eyes narrowed at Beanie. "I'd say she's more like Susan LaFlesche Picotte—" He dropped his gaze, taking in my hand wrapped around Nash's wrist before his eyes flashed up to mine with a soft smile. "The first female Native American doctor," he added. "Why don't we get you kids a drink? Excuse us, Beanie, Brad."

Beanie shuffled out of the way, seeming to realize his misstep as Nash continued to glare at him. My excitement faded as Steve cast another look at Nash and me, his gaze troubled. Had I ruined Nash's time here with his father?

Would the rest of the band find me as nerdy and weird as this Beanie fellow?

Nash seemed so at home in this room, with these people. But I wasn't comfortable, and I realized I'd been right to worry. I would never be comfortable with these people—in this room.

What had I gotten myself into?

It was just a week. I could do anything for a week… Then I'd be in Boston, with like-minded teens preparing for the next phase of their life.

And Nash… He fit here. This was his world.

But it would never be mine.

Chapter 12
Nash

I didn't like Aya's silence or her attempts to fade into the background. So I came out swinging, like I always did in these situations.

I stormed up to Beanie. "Why did you upset Aya?"

Beanie sneered. "Why do you even care? She's just some chick. I hope you're banging that at least."

"She's *my friend*," I stressed. "I invited her…"

Beanie narrowed his eyes. "And this is *my* band. If you're going to continue to be a little shit, I'll be sure you get sent home."

I clenched my fists but kept my mouth shut. No way my dad would let Beanie talk to me like that. After their show, I'd tell him. He'd deal with Beanie.

He'd better.

Steve settled into the space nearby, waiting for me to calm down.

"What?" I snapped at him.

"Maybe Aya doesn't belong here," Steve said. "Maybe this simply won't be her scene."

"Bullshit," I spat. "She likes hanging out with me."

Steve rocked his head back, almost as if he couldn't believe I'd yelled at him. I couldn't believe it either, but I kept the concern that Beanie might throw us out locked down tight. Steve might be one of the few adults I could trust, but that didn't give him the right to pick on Aya.

He sighed. "You *really* like her."

"I do."

Steve rubbed the back of his neck. "You're young, so you don't see the dangers ahead. Just as you can't see how much you mean to each other—how much you need each other. That girl… I get it, Nash. She's special. Smart, caring, and beautiful."

I growled, and Steve smirked. "She's also seventeen, and I'm old enough to be her father." He blanched.

I crossed my arms over my chest. *What did that have to do with anything?*

A little while later, I settled next to Aya as Quantum took the stage. She clasped her hands under her chin, and her eyes shone with excitement. When my dad started the opening chords for one of his most popular songs, Aya gasped, her eyes going wide.

I smiled, loving that I shared this first with her.

When my dad gave me the cue, Aya threw her arms around me and whispered good luck in my ear. I turned my head and pressed my lips to hers. The moment seemed to slow, then stop. Her lips were soft, plump, perfect. She pulled back, a shy smile teasing her mouth.

"Get out there," she said.

I nearly stumbled as I made my way onto the stage. A roadie handed me my guitar, and I settled in next to my dad.

"Hey, Dallas. This is my son, Nash."

Dad squeezed my shoulder and grinned as the crowd went wild. "He's going to play this next song with me since he had a hand in crafting it."

Dad continued the chords, and I kept up, just like we'd practiced. He began the song but backed off after the first chorus, letting me sing the last two verses. The crowd went nuts, their screams filling my head with joy.

This high—it was *amazing*. I glanced over at Aya and winked.

She stood there, mesmerized. She didn't move or even seem to blink. But she clapped and cheered with the rest of the audience when I took my bow. I ran off the stage to people screaming my name. I lifted her from the ground and spun her around, nearly tripping over the various cords on the floor.

"You were awesome," she squealed, which turned into a laugh.

I laughed too, loving that she'd been here to see me.

Still onstage, Dad segued into another tune as the roadie took my guitar.

Aya turned to me, swaying, eyes wide. "I can see why you're into live music."

I grimaced. "Not so much this song."

"Not one of yours?"

I shook my head. "No, thank fuck."

She giggled.

We listened to another couple of songs, but the magical moment was gone. The band played hard, but they'd lost the crowd. Dad shot me an angry look, so I leaned over toward Aya.

"Want to head back to the hotel?"

She nodded.

We walked out of the venue, followed by Steve, and I sighed out some of the tension I'd been carrying in my shoulders since the run-in earlier with Beanie.

"So what did you think about the concert?" I asked. "Better than climbing the side of a mountain?"

She scrunched her brow as Steve opened the car door and motioned us in. "Better…" She shrugged. "At least the first part. Your songs are exhilarating."

I smiled. "Yeah, there's nothing like being part of a live concert."

She shook her head. "No, I meant your songs, Nash. It's easy to tell which ones you wrote."

I caught Steve's look in the rearview mirror and sucked in my lips to keep from smiling like a damn fool.

"Thanks."

Aya shrugged. "It's the truth." She sighed as she turned toward the window. "You'll be up there with millions of fans screaming for *you* soon."

I gripped her hand. "And you'll be backstage, ready to tell me how awesome I am."

She smiled as she rested her head on my shoulder. "I'm glad I got to see this."

Something in her voice worried me. But before I could ask her about it, we arrived at the hotel. Instead of hanging out in the suite's living room with Steve and me, Aya excused herself, claiming she needed to call her mom.

I stared at her closed bedroom door, dread creeping up my spine. "You're right," I said.

"I'm always right," Steve said with a grin. But at my worried look, his face smoothed out. "What's wrong?"

"She doesn't like touring."

Steve's expression turned pensive. He cleared his throat. "Could be she doesn't like Beanie."

"Neither do I."

Steve hesitated for a moment. "Say the word, and I'll get you home."

"Not happening," I said, tone flat. "I'm supposed to keep performing with Dad."

Except I didn't.

"The roadies lost your guitar," Dad said at the next show.

"I'll just borrow—"

"No. You're not playing tonight." He turned away.

With each show, my father's temper frayed further, and I started to understand the problem. When reporters asked Dad how many of his songs I'd helped write, he snapped out that I'd helped him with a few words, his eyes dark and daring me to contradict him.

I kept my mouth shut, hoping he'd let me play again.

More critics panned the new album and the tour, sending Dad into a rage. He smashed tables in the green room that night, and Steve whisked Aya and me out of there. We ended up at a barbecue joint before heading to the movies. While fun, it wasn't what I'd expected. And as pissed as Dad was, I was equally as frustrated that he'd lied to me, and to the media.

Instead of sold-out arenas, Quantum's ticket sales had declined by the end of the first week as we moved on to Nashville.

When I finally found a moment to tell my father what Beanie had said, he nodded. "Too right. Don't be a shit, Nash."

I rocked back on my heels, gaping before I managed to say, "But—"

"But nothing," Dad snapped loud enough for everyone in the green room to hear.

My ears burned, but I held his gaze. Why was he being such a dick? Dad sauntered in closer, using his additional thirty pounds to bump me back.

"Remember, you had nothing to do with this album or this tour. *Nothing.* If you want to stay with me, you'd better treat the band and the rest of the staff with respect."

He turned and walked away—straight into the arms of a woman with red-slicked lips and thick eyeliner, giving her a cat-like look. She glanced at me briefly before pressing her body against my father's.

Aya inched closer to me, no doubt feeling my shudder of revulsion.

Steve laid his hands on our shoulders. "Time to head to the hotel," he said.

Neither of us argued.

Later that night, after the concert, Aya was in her room reading some thick, boring book about an astronaut that she claimed was fascinating. I'd left her to hang out with my dad in his suite—at his request. The July heat pressed against my skin as we stood on the balcony, making it itch a bit, but I wasn't focused on the physical discomfort. Instead, I gaped up at my father, still unsteady from the bombshell he'd dropped.

"You don't want me on tour with you?" I asked.

I couldn't believe his words. No way! *No way* my father didn't want me… I'd pretty much written Quantum's previous album; my dad had promised to take me to the concerts, to let me hear the fans' reactions to *my* songs. To let me play one of them, tell the world they were mine.

"But you said…" I couldn't finish the sentence. My ears rang as embarrassment crested over me in a huge wave.

He refused to look at me, instead facing the Nashville skyline and clutching the thick, metal railing. "This tour's based on the collaboration between Beanie and me because you wouldn't write anything."

"Because I couldn't—" I swallowed. "I've been busy with school…"

"Anyway, there's really no reason for you to join me on this next leg."

"But you said I could play my song—"

Dad tossed his half-smoked cigarette off the balcony, not seeming to care where it landed below. Smoke rippled out of his nose. "Those are my songs. *Mine*. They're on my album, and my band plays them."

"I wrote them, and you said I could play—"

Dad narrowed his light brown eyes, and I felt a twinge of unease. "No. You're not going to fuck with my music. My legacy."

"But…but…"

Dad kicked at my lounger. "You're fucking up my band. You need to go home in the morning. Get your mom to spend time with you."

"Mom's in Paris."

"Like I give a fuck. Stay here, hang out with that little girl you brought along. I don't care as long as you're not with me."

Those words slammed hard into my chest, reverberating there, much as the metal lounger continued to vibrate from Dad's kick. The thick, fluffy cushion couldn't conceal the attack.

If I hadn't been sitting, I might have staggered backward under the onslaught of emotions. The physicality and the ugly, closed expression on Dad's face combined with the words… I felt as if he'd hit me, not once but many times. My chest felt bruised and achy.

I swallowed a deep sense of loss. I'd prided myself on my easy relationship with my father. But I realized now, that had been gone since Lev died.

I had to try one more time. "Dad, I don't understand…"

His face twisted in a snarl, and I shrank from him, unsure if I should run or prepare for a blow.

"Are you stupid?" he yelled. "I said no, you're not performing. You're not part of my tour. That's the end of it."

Silence engulfed us. I felt…bereft, as I had when Lev died. I could hear Dad breathing in sharp pants. The door opened behind me, and my neck prickled as Steve came to stand next to me. He kept his gaze on my father, and something passed between them.

"I don't have time for this shit," Dad said, pushing past Steve and striding through the suite.

"Are you okay?" Steve asked. Worry clouded his eyes.

I was contemplating how to form words when my phone rang. I pulled it out of my pocket. Cam's smiling face appeared on the screen for a video call, and I pressed the green Accept button, feeling wooden.

Cam's grin slid off his face. "What's wrong?"

I blinked back tears. "My dad just told me I can't travel with him for the rest of the tour."

Cam turned his head away, jaw jutting. After a long pause, he turned back, anger in his eyes. "He give you a reason?"

"He…he said…he said he didn't care where I ended up as long as it wasn't with him." My lip quivered, and I felt tears in my eyes. I swiped at them, angry and embarrassed. They couldn't fall—that would make my humiliation complete.

"Because of the songs," Cam muttered, so low I nearly missed his words. He cleared his throat as he popped a Werther's into his mouth. "Your dad reminds me too much of my own old man. And that makes me sorry for us both."

I hadn't gone over to the Graces' ranch when Cam's dad was around because I didn't like the way Mr. Grace spoke to Cam. It was too much like how my dad spoke to me. He'd been angry since he realized I'd helped Cam with that song, reminding me that composing music was our thing and that "*it's all in the family*." I guess that meant I wasn't supposed to tell other musicians or something. But it's not like Cam went around blabbing about me. Though, come to think of it, Cam had been annoyed that my father hadn't credited me on his albums.

I didn't know what to say to Cam's comment. And I didn't like having Steve witness my blubbering. Embarrassment scalded me yet again, and I shrugged. "Whatever." I sniffled and turned my face away. I shouldn't have accepted this call. But then I'd be talking to Steve, who still stood in the doorway, his face stiff and unhappy.

"Where are you?" Cam asked.

"We rolled into Nashville today."

"I'll be there tomorrow. You can tour with me. I'll talk to your mom—"

"She's in Europe," I said, my voice sounding like someone else's. *"Are you stupid?"* My father's words swirled through my head.

Cam grunted. "Well, then I guess it won't be a problem for you to hang out with me."

I turned so I could watch the moonlight glisten over the river. It wasn't too distant, and it reminded me a little of the lake back home. Aya said that was the prettiest time of night, right after moonrise. Tonight, though, it didn't calm me. I wanted to rest my head on Aya's shoulder. I wanted Steve or Cam to hug me.

"Great," I told him. "Sounds fabulous." I shoved my foot along the expensive tile, liking the slick feel under my shoe. "But you have better things to do than hang out with me—"

"Like I've said before, you remind me of me, but with more talent. Plus, the reason I called was to tell you Asher Smith wants to meet you. He saw your song that first night." Cam cleared his throat. "Yeah, so he asked about you. He knows you helped me with 'Sweet Baby Home'."

My eyes widened. "Asher Smith?"

Cam grinned. "Isn't he your hero?"

A reluctant smile tugged at my lips. "*You* are if I can hang out with him."

Cam laughed. "Consider it done."

"Seriously?" My head felt light, my body giddy. Asher Smith *and* Camden Grace. Those guys were way bigger than Quantum. Holy hell.

Take that, Dad.

In that moment, I decided I'd never write another song for my father again. He wanted to call me stupid? Tell me he didn't want me around? *Fine*. My songs would be mine. Or for people I chose to give them to, not someone who demanded them.

Cam's gaze darted up toward Steve, who stood over me like a damn Roman sentinel.

"Tell you what, why don't you see if your friend—what's her name?" Cam asked.

"Aya."

"Cool. Ask her if she wants to come, and you'll both join my entourage tomorrow. Steve, can you get the kids to the venue tomorrow afternoon? Say three o'clock?"

"Of course. As long as it's okay with Aya's mother."

"Can't imagine I'm a worse role model than Brad's been," Cam muttered.

I had to agree with him. Dad seemed to go out of his way to make Aya uncomfortable.

"Maybe we can collaborate on another song," Cam said. "And you can sing it onstage."

The swell of excitement in my belly crashed as I realized what Cam was doing. "I don't want your pity. That's what this is. You feel sorry for me."

He shook his head. "You know we released 'Sweet Baby Home' first. The song *you* wrote. And do you know why?"

Warmth rippled over my skin like a caress. "Nope."

"Because it's the best song on the album, Nash. That's saying something, because I'm a hella good songwriter. But *your* song is better, and it's going to blow me into the stratosphere."

"All right. If you really think the song's good enough…"

"It definitely is," Cam said, his tone warm. "Asher thinks so, too. So, we'll need to get you two together. We'll talk more about that tomorrow."

I nodded, and as I ended the call, I felt calmer, almost happy.

Until I remembered my dad's comments.

"Do you…hear music in your head?" Steve asked after a moment.

I shrugged. "Sometimes."

"New melodies or other people's songs?" he asked, his tone a bit urgent.

Weird change of topic. I felt a strange flutter in my belly. It was a tangled mix of dark emotions I couldn't quite tease apart.

I frowned. "Some of both, I guess."

"Let's…ah, let's get you back to your room," he said. "We'll get everything sorted out tomorrow." He cleared his throat and patted my shoulder in an awkward show of affection.

"You don't have to feel bad for me," I muttered as I stood.

"I don't feel bad. I, uh, I think what you can do is a gift. You're…you're one in a million, kid."

I stared up at the stars for a moment, wishing my father had said those words to me. Then I followed Steve back through the suite and out the door.

Chapter 13
Aya

When Nash returned to the suite and told me about the change of plans, I felt my entire body unclench, and I breathed a sigh I hadn't realized I'd been holding in.

"Okay." I studied him. "Are you sure you're okay with this? I mean…you want to do this?"

Nash nodded, some of the disappointment clearing from his features. "Oh, yeah. Cam said I could collaborate with him, perform."

His excitement caused me to smile, even as my stomach tightened again. I hated the idea of going out onstage, and I couldn't imagine a worse experience than having thousands of eyes trained on me, expecting musical perfection. I suppressed a shudder.

Nash stood from his chair and stretched. "Want to watch something?"

I smiled and scooted over on the bed, my belly flipping as a thin slice of his tanned stomach flashed into view. I patted the space next to me, my mouth too dry to speak.

"Ay?"

"You pick." I smiled as I handed him the remote from the bedside table, trying to regulate my breathing.

He plopped onto the bed and shoved another pillow behind

his back. Just then Steve poked his head through the connecting door, a frown on his face. He opened his mouth and I tensed, ready for him to tell Nash to come back to their room.

But his gaze softened as he watched Nash wiggle into a comfortable position, toeing off his shoes. Steve's gaze met mine, and I read the concern there, as well as a stern demand to behave. I nodded and settled back against the pillows, keeping space between Nash and me.

"I'll leave the door open so you can come to bed when you finish your show," Steve said.

"Sure." Nash nodded, never taking his eyes from the screen as he flicked through the options. "Oooh, look, Ay, they got the new horror flick."

I shuddered even as I sighed in acquiescence. It wasn't that horror films terrified me—they didn't—but I wasn't big into gore, and that was Nash's preference. Still, something about him seemed off tonight, and he needed this. I'd just have to close my eyes against all the blood.

Steve sent me a sympathetic look as he leaned against the door frame, and my concern for Nash ratcheted up. But then Nash pressed play, so I settled in.

Steve finally stopped hovering in the doorway about halfway through the movie. The next scene proved even grosser than the previous ones, and I buried my face in Nash's chest. His arm came around my shoulder, and he patted me in an absent way that told me he was deeply engrossed. I sighed and closed my eyes, relaxing against his side.

I must have fallen asleep, because the next thing I knew, the credits were rolling. Nash shifted, trying to reach the lamp, which was on the other side of me.

He glanced down and noted my opened eyes. His seemed stormy, his unguarded face filled with anguish.

"What's wrong?" I asked.

His jaw clenched so hard, I heard his teeth clack together. Maybe I lifted my palm and cupped his cheek because I was still half asleep. Or maybe not… I rubbed my thumb over his lip. His breath puffed against my skin, and I shivered as the tension eased from his body.

He wrapped his arms around me, pulling me flush against him. His hands splayed wider, covering more of me as he rolled over, pressing me into the mattress. My hips cradled his, my arms twining around his neck, slithering into his hair.

"Nash," I whispered. "What is it?

"My dad doesn't want me here," he said.

"Well, your father is a jealous idiot."

"You told me that months ago."

I nodded. "I remember."

Brad's comments must have cut deep. I understood that all too well. I leaned up and kissed him, pulling back quickly, though I didn't want to. "I'm sorry."

He rested his forehead against the side of my neck, and I shivered as his lips brushed the sensitive skin there. I cuddled closer. He pressed his hips forward, bumping against my leggings and the soft flesh beneath—a question. I opened my legs wider, wanting him, wanting this.

"Aya…" he murmured. He rose up on his elbows, brushing

the hair from my forehead. I tipped my head in invitation, and he leaned down, our breath mingling.

We tensed at the sound of footfalls coming toward the open doorway. Nash flopped onto his back next to me, turning his head on the pillow. I lay there, sprawled, heart thumping, cursing Steve.

Nash's gaze cut to the door. "I'm coming to bed in a sec."

"All right," Steve said. "Goodnight, Aya."

My smile trembled but I managed, "Goodnight."

Nash cleared his throat. "When do you leave?"

I bit my lip. "I can stay through Sunday." That was three days from now. "There's a flight out Sunday evening. It's a red-eye…"

"So after the show?" he asked, hopeful.

"I..."

He rose up on his elbow and used his free hand to press his finger to my lips. "Trust me, Ay. If you stay for the show, I'll get you to Boston."

Chapter 14
Nash

The next afternoon, Camden Grace strode into the green room at Bridgestone Arena after his sound check, his dark hair messy and a bit damp. He'd played the Grand Ole Opry the night before, but tonight was a much larger show—in terms of both seats and tech—than the intimate version. His eyes flitted around, taking in not just the people in the room, but the furniture, the exits… everything. He pulled a Werther's from his pocket and popped it in his mouth. Cam's longtime head of security, Chuck, followed a step behind. A deep scowl settled on Chuck's face, causing him to look even burlier.

Their gazes turned to Aya and me, and Aya shrank back a couple of inches, easing behind me. No doubt she worried this reception would be like what she'd gotten from Beanie last week. But I felt myself shaking with excitement.

Cam held out his hand as he walked toward me, smiling, some of the darkness lifting from his eyes. "Nash. It's good to have you 'round again."

His voice was low, smoky but smooth. A new tune popped into my head, and I struggled not to hum it aloud as we shook. Excitement licked over my skin as more of the melody flowed, smooth as glass, through my head.

"We missed you at the recording sessions for the rest of the album," he noted. "You'll have to give me your opinion now, though I could have used it then."

"I was hanging out with Aya," I said with a shrug.

Cam's gaze slid over my shoulder. His smile turned gentle. "And you're Aya?"

She squeaked a little as she stepped forward. "Yes, sir."

Cam chuckled. "None of that sir business, now. I decommissioned a while back and plan to keep it that way." He winked as he offered his hand.

She took it, and I felt that same weird, intense feeling bubble up in my belly. I didn't like Cam looking at Aya. I didn't like him holding her hand... What the hell was wrong with me?

My world seemed to spin off axis a little as Steve's words from the other day looped through my head, knocking out the melody. *"You're young, so you don't see the dangers ahead. Just as you can't see how much you mean to each other—how much you need each other."*

I *did* need Aya. Besides Cam and Steve, she was the only true person in my life. The one constant I could count on, who'd be there for me. Why was that bad?

Cam let go of Aya's hand, which eased some of the tension in my chest, but they were now discussing horses.

"Your sister might like the Jumli," Aya said. "It's the most prevalent horse in Nepal. It's a bit small, though, and used for work—not unlike barrel racing, if your sister does that."

Cam shook his head. "Nah. Katie Rose likes to ride fast, but she never loved the routes. I heard about another breed... Marwari, is it?"

Aya nodded. "Oh, yes, but they're actually from India." She tucked her hair behind her ear and frowned. "Sorry, that's rather a technicality. Those horses are beautiful and fast."

Cam leaned in a little. "Tell me everything you know. I gotta make sure I have the intel to pass along to my mama and sister."

Aya smiled up at him—her shy one that blossomed slowly. Cam seemed as charmed as most of the boys at school. My hands fisted. *Dammit.* Bringing Aya along had been a bad idea. First Beanie was mean, and now…now Cam seemed to like her.

I gritted my teeth, unsure what to do with the emotions tumbling through my middle like I'd hit class-five rapids without warning.

Then Chuck asked Aya a question. She became more animated, using her hands as she spoke, and he leaned in, too.

Good, she wasn't star-struck. So maybe she wouldn't crush on Cam like so many of the girls at Holyoke did. According to them, Cam was gorgeous and talented, and they always hoped the young, single singer would look their way.

I settled back against the wall, watching Aya interact with the world's biggest country star. Part of me was proud of her easy connection with Camden Grace, especially since the man intimidated me. But another part felt left out.

Steve took up position next to me. "Chuck doesn't talk to anyone."

I glanced over, eyebrow raised. "Evidently he talks to Aya. Why did you say we can't see the trouble coming?"

Steve rubbed his hand over his neck, seeming uncomfortable. "I was in love once," he said.

"All right..." Not what I expected, but I guessed he'd get somewhere interesting soon.

"She was older. Incredibly beautiful. Charming, playful." He smiled, but it was sad.

My brows pinched. "What happened?"

"She had other priorities, and I still had a few years left in the Army." His eyes turned distant. "Didn't matter how much I wanted to be part of her world, how willing I was to rearrange my life to suit hers."

"Is she a model?" I asked. "From what I've seen, they're the most selfish."

"You thinking about your mom?" Steve asked.

I shrugged.

"Look, my point was, I met her when I was nineteen—too young to have a good sense of how I was messing up my life by trying to be what *she* wanted. I got...caught up in the romance, in the highs of spending time with her." He hesitated. "Is that how you feel about Aya?"

I placed my heel against the wall and stared at Aya, considering. "Not really. I met her for the first time when we were five. She was in trouble in the water."

Steve cursed low.

"I pulled her out, and the way she looked at me..." No other event in my life had made me feel that way since. I cleared my throat. "But it was more than that. We...I don't know. I didn't even know her when we started corresponding. Not really. Just a vague sense of a little girl I'd met on vacation. But we connected. I *know* her. She gets me. It's like...

it's like our lives have run parallel to each other from that moment."

"Seems kind of deep for a girlfriend."

I snorted, hoping I wasn't blushing, though my face felt too hot not to be. "You know Aya's not my girlfriend. It's not like that."

This time Steve snorted.

"She understands about drowning," I tried to explain. "Lev drowned. Her dad is a shit bag, and so is mine. She's losing control of her life—mine's been out of control since Lev..."

Steve's hand came down on my shoulder, and he squeezed. "I get it," he said, his voice soft. "She's *more* than a girlfriend."

I nodded, but I also struggled to swallow. Because I'd realized something as I spoke. Aya was more than a girlfriend could *ever* be. She looked over at me, making sure I was here, making sure I was okay.

That's why I'd connected with her so seamlessly. That's why I felt best in her presence.

She was my other half.

Chapter 15
Aya

I'd thought Quantum put on an amazing show. But now, after watching Cam and his band power through three days of performances in a sold-out venue, one of the country's largest stadiums, I understood greatness. I waited in the wings, breath bated, along with the tens of thousands of people packed into the stadium as Cam stood—clad in his typical attire of a black button-up, faded but crisp jeans, and motorcycle boots—in front of his mic.

He stood there…waiting, waiting, waiting. The collective tension rose. And then, when it reached fever pitch, Cam leaned closer to the mic and began to croon "Sweet Baby Home"—the song he and Nash had collaborated on. The lyrics were filled with need and anguish for a woman thousands of miles from the soldier. It made my chest ache each time I heard it, but hearing it live—Cam's strong, deep voice low, sultry, and a cappella—made the hairs on my arms and the back of my neck stand on end. All the air rushed from my lungs as he eased into the chorus.

Lights flashed as he and his band began to play, the first strum of the guitar and beat of the snare a relief from the building tension. I sagged against Nash, who practically vibrated with energy. When he turned, his eyes were huge as they met mine.

"That was unreal," he yelled as the crowd burst into applause.

He turned back to face the stage, which was now lit with a

variety of lights. They cast shadows over Nash's features as Cam waved him onto the stage. Tonight, it was time. Cam had kept his promise.

"This is Nash Porter. He co-wrote this song with me," Cam told the crowd. "I wanted y'all to meet him cuz he's a superstar."

Cam winked, and Nash rocked back on his heels, flashing his gaze toward me. I giggled even as my heart cracked a little. That had been my private joke with Nash, but now others would call him that. Still, it was worth it to watch him light up so brightly as he stepped out into the glow of the stage. He belonged there.

Nash accepted the guitar a roadie offered him and stepped up to the microphone. "Hey, Nashville. Like your name."

The crowd screamed its approval.

"Y'all wanna see what this guy can do?" Cam asked. He began to play a complicated series of licks, which Nash matched with a smirk. That told me they'd done this before.

Cam began to sing and dipped his head toward the mic. Nash harmonized, and my jaw dropped. Steve's typical implacable expression shifted to one of awe as Nash balanced and emphasized Cam's voice, the two of them feeding off each other. By the end, the crowd's screams were so loud, I covered my ears.

Nash took his bow, waving and smiling as the raucous cheers continued. He walked toward me, grin bigger than the Cheshire cat, and swung me into his arms and then around.

"You were amazing," I said, clasping his cheeks. "Really, Superstar."

His smile turned shy. "I like it better when you say that."

He set me on my feet, and I rose up on my tiptoes to kiss

him. I looked into his eyes, not even caring that Steve was probably staring at us. "And I'm so glad I was here to see you perform, Nash Porter. My superstar."

He beamed as he wrapped an arm around my waist and tugged me back against his chest. I was cocooned—warm, protected. Loved.

He might not admit it, but Nash cared about me, about my approval. Too bad I had to leave. I bit my lip, wondering if I'd made a mistake. My mother had left the final decision in my hands, surprising me.

"*You live once, Aya. I don't want you to have regrets*," she'd told me when I spoke with her earlier.

"I'm glad you were here," Nash murmured against my cheek. I leaned against his chest and he braced his feet on the outsides of mine. His arms wrapped around my waist and his breath tickled the hairs around my ear.

I tipped my head back, noting how close his lips were to mine. I wanted them *on* mine. I wanted him to admit his feelings. I wanted…more than Nash was ready to give—maybe more than he would ever give me.

"Why?" I asked.

"Because as much as I like performing, it's personal. Well, not so much this song because Cam already had the lyrics written, but other ones. My songs. They're…" He clutched me tighter. "I'm just glad you're here. It's easier to sing with you nearby."

Not a declaration of love, but still an opening. Nash was more truthful with me than he was with just about anyone else. And still I struggled to know what he thought, how he felt.

Part of that was being the son of famous parents, but a larger part was due to the trauma inflicted by his parents' choices. They'd abandoned him right when he needed them most. No one overcame that type of pain with ease or without it changing something fundamental inside. I knew this from experience.

But I refused to think of my own father. This was Nash's night, and I'd bask in the connection between us.

We watched the rest of Cam's show like that. Afterward, Cam insisted on taking us out for a celebratory milkshake, and then he packed up his bus while Steve waited nearby in the SUV we'd used to get our drinks.

"See you in Atlanta," Cam said, giving Nash a fist bump. He turned and wrapped me in a hug. "And give those Boston boys hell."

Nash scowled.

"Thank you for having me—" I began.

"None of that," Cam said. "You're welcome on my tour anytime, Aya. Plus, you make that sad sack over there smile." He leaned in closer and murmured, "I like that boy happy."

"Me, too."

Nash and Steve then drove me to the airport. When we arrived, Steve pulled around to a private hangar at the back and up to a sleek white jet with the logo for Syad Hotel Group on the side.

"We're flying private?" I asked.

"Of course," Nash said. "It just sits in the hangar in Austin most of the time. I figured this was a good use of it. We can get you up to Boston and then meet Cam in Atlanta—and we can all catch some sleep."

"That's so thoughtful," I said, my shock morphing into warmth.

He tucked a tendril of hair behind my ear, rubbing the strands. "I'm glad you stayed tonight, Aya. It meant a lot to me. So, yeah, I'm going to make sure you get to your nerd class as rested as possible."

I laughed even as I smacked his arm. "I thought I was smart and badass."

"You are. The rest..." Nash trailed off, scowling.

"Let's get you on board," Steve said. "The pilot's gone through his flight check and is ready to go."

The flight felt short, mainly because I fell asleep within moments of take-off. I woke to find Nash's head atop mine and his hand over mine, which rested on his upper thigh. Another few inches and I'd...

Nash snorted, and I giggled. He lifted his head, eyes bleary. I sat up and noted Steve's gaze on us. I hoped I didn't blush. Thank goodness I hadn't acted on my impulse. Then I sighed, realizing I didn't even know what I was to Nash—and that he was going to be with all the pretty girls along the East Coast for the next few weeks.

"Why don't you two go clean up and change?" Steve suggested. His hair was damp, so he must have already used the facilities. "We have some time before Aya's check-in."

Nash took my hand and led me out the door of the plane. I blinked, still fuzzy from sleep, surprised to see the sun was up. He smiled. "The flight was only a couple of hours, so Steve had the pilot take the scenic route."

I shook my head. "The amount of fuel—"

"Leave it, Aya. It's done. You needed rest. So did I." He cleared his throat. "Steve said he'd record the concerts. I could send those to you."

I grabbed his hand, tugging him against my chest. I noted the way his pupils expanded and his nostrils flared. Nash liked my chest. A lot. "I'd be happy to watch your performances," I said as we climbed into the waiting SUV.

"Breakfast, then to MIT," Steve said, sliding into the driver's seat.

"Any place you want to go?" Nash asked.

I shrugged. "Not sure."

"Steve did some research," Nash said.

We ate at a little diner not far from the main campus, and Nash insisted I take a chai to go. After we arrived, he walked me to the registration table, his gaze keen as he took in the old trees and towering white buildings.

Steve stood to the side while I checked in.

The woman at the desk smiled at me, a polite show of teeth. "And who's this?"

"Oh, Nash is my friend," I said. I clutched the welcome packet she handed me as another couple of girls and six teenaged boys broke off from the back.

"Are you Aya?" one of the girls asked.

I nodded, stepping closer to Nash.

"I'm Li. You're on our team. We've been waiting for you."

"Oh. Well, hi—"

"We need to start looking at plans for our robotics entry," Li said.

"I need to head to the dorms. I haven't dropped my luggage—"

"No, we need to start now," Li said. "All the other teams are already brainstorming." She waved her hand at the clusters of teenagers sprawled around the large room.

I turned to face Nash, not ready to let him go.

He slid a lanyard with my name tag over my head. "Steve and I will get your luggage to your room," he said. Then he sighed. "I'm going to miss you."

"Is this your boyfriend?" Li asked.

For the first time, she didn't sound bossy. She sounded envious.

"Yeah, I am," Nash said, eyeing the boys in the group. "Be sure to tell the others she's taken."

I looked up, a question on my lips, but Nash bent down and kissed me. He wrapped me tightly in his arms, just as he had last night and sealed his mouth over mine. I parted my lips, needing more, but he pulled back, clearly aware of our audience. *Right.* My cheeks flamed.

"I'm going to hold you to your promise about the shows. And I mean it—I want you to be mine," he murmured in my ear.

I tipped my head back, holding his gaze. My worry about the girls he'd meet over the next weeks faded as I noted his proprietary glare around the room. Nash had just staked his claim. In front of my entire summer cohort.

Instead of being frustrated with his high-handedness, I melted. Because he was jealous. Because he couldn't stand the idea of me hooking up with an MIT boy any more than I could handle him with one of the beautiful fans.

Nash glowered for a moment longer, and then he smiled at me—the devastating one that made me hot and bothered—before he walked over to Steve.

Another girl in our group sidled up to me. “Your boyfriend’s hot.”

“He is.” I nodded, my gaze still trailing Nash.

“He seemed to want to make sure no one here bothered you,” she said.

I finally turned to look at her. “What’s your name?” I asked.

“Sarai,” she said.

I offered her my hand. “Aya.”

“Oh, we all know who you are now,” she said with a laugh. “You’re the girl with the hot boyfriend.”

Well, there were worse ways to be known.

Chapter 16
Nash

As I returned to Atlanta and Cam's tour without Aya, I moped. Having Aya with me had reminded me of my days touring with Lev. We were a team, together, sharing experiences. Now, once again, I was alone.

Maybe I shouldn't have pushed for more than friendship with her. I wanted her—wanted the MIT nerds to know she was mine—but I'd watched my parents' relationship shatter many times. What if I'd pushed the friendship I cherished into a place where it was doomed to fail?

Still, despite my second-guessing, I missed her, no matter how much Cam tried to cheer me up. I had used the plane ride from Boston to Atlanta and then the hours at the venue to compose three tunes, though—the first I'd managed in *years*.

Cam whistled as he read them, his head bobbing to the melody. "These're damn fine." He settled back in his chair in this newest suite in yet another fancy hotel. "Why don't you work one of these tunes up real good and you can sing it in a couple of weeks all by yourself? That's after we do 'Sweet Baby Home', though."

I gasped. "You'd let me do that? Take over part of your set?"

"Sure. My fans are gonna love you."

Excitement caused me to twitch in my spot on the couch, but I frowned. "I, uh… I'm not sure I'm country-music material."

Cam smirked. “You do have a bit of an edge to you.”

“So…wouldn’t one of these songs dilute your brand?”

He leaned back. “Nope. My fans like me because I got an edge to me, too. Think about what music is doing, Nash. It’s evolving, right? Pushing boundaries, blending.” He leaned forward and flicked the music still clutched in my hands. “These walk a line between rock and country, and there seems to be an appetite for that. I mean, I’m there a lot of the time.”

I stared down at the lined paper in my lap, then swallowed and looked up. “Why are you so nice to me?”

Cam smirked. “Because I can be.”

I began to frown.

“No,” he said. “You’re not here out of pity.” He popped a Werther’s into his mouth, his eyes burning with intensity. “I told you before, your father reminds me of mine.” He glanced away, his jaw clenching. “Maybe if my old man had spent some of his time helping me instead of disparaging me, things would have been different.” His sentence ended softly, as if he were admitting that to himself for the first time.

“I’m just a kid—”

“With talent. And kindness. My mama likes you. Once I told her about you, back when I lived next door, she tasked me to look out for you because she worried about your influences, since your parents…”

I stared at my Converse sneakers. “Since my parents pretty much abandoned me.”

Fuck. I hated that I was like Lord Prescott in any way. But… truth was, whether it hurt or not. And this truth cut deep. My parents had given up on me when Lev died. And my subconscious had known long before I was willing to admit my family had shattered. There was no fixing it. I hated Dad for that, almost as much as I hated myself. Because my father might be selfish, but I'd been the one who didn't fulfill my role, didn't write songs when he needed them. And now, my family would never heal. *So fuck it.*

I clutched the music I'd just written. I'd wanted this—the ability to create something perfect—for so long. And now that passion flared brighter because these songs were for *me.* My father had made his point the other night. There was no going back. I was done.

"Look, Nash. You've had some hard knocks," Cam said, interrupting my thoughts. "I get that. Also think you're talented. And a good man." He smirked at my scoff. "You're ready to fly. I got the connections and ability to make that happen. Plus, I happen to like you."

"Don't forget your pay-it-forward theory," Chuck rumbled.

I glanced over at Cam's head of security, frowning.

Cam nodded. "Right. I help you now; you help someone else when the time's right. Maybe multiple someones. One thing I learned in the Army—we do a lot of damage, but we rarely try to fix underlying issues. In your case, I can give you the opportunities your father should be giving you. It's a song, an introduction. It's hanging out with you. And it's nothing hard since I'm more than glad to do all that."

I smoothed the pages over my lap. "Like…a mentor?" I asked, still wrapping my mind around Cam's kindness.

"Yep. Like that. And one day, I'll be begging you to take my calls." He laughed.

I clenched my hands into fists. "That'll never happen."

Cam sobered. "Back to the song. You down?"

I considered it a moment. "Yeah. Yeah, I'd like that. Can…can we time it so I play close to Boston?"

"Damn straight. How about Madison Square Garden? That's in a little over a month. Call up your girl. Get her to fly out for the show."

I swallowed, all my emotions about Aya bombarding me once again. "What about you? Have you—"

He waved his hand. "I don't talk about my past. Because that's all it is."

I nodded, unsure how to respond.

"Well, go on, then," he said.

But his face didn't seem as relaxed as his voice. I'd struck a nerve with my attempted question.

He pulled another Werther's from his pocket and popped it in his mouth. "Pick out your favorite and get to practicing."

When Aya called that night, her tension and sadness permeated the screen. This morning, she'd looked nervous as we left, but excited. Tonight—so late it was already morning again—she was different.

"What's wrong?" I asked.

Her lower lip quivered, and she looked away. "Nothing."

"Aya…"

She closed her eyes. "It's just… I'm not sure I made the right choice, coming here. Li's been…" She blew out a breath, opened her eyes, and smiled. But I could see the strain. "I miss you."

"Yeah. Today sucked without you here," I said. I flopped down on the bed, shifting pillows to get comfortable. "Tell me about your day."

And then she did, eyes alight with purpose. *Fuck*. How could I have missed how important this was to her? Like she'd said, STEM for her was like music to me. A solid weight pressed against my chest.

"What did you do?" she asked when she finished telling me about Li and their project and came up for air.

"We're getting ready for the show tomorrow."

"Right." She bathed that lower lip with her tongue. That drove me nuts. "That's all?"

I opened my mouth, but she was so into her program… Was it fair of me to pull her attention away from her passion? Just to get her to share mine?

"Not much else to tell," I said, managing a smile. "You're well aware that tours aren't as glamorous as people think."

We clicked off soon after, and I felt restless, unhappy. Steve was in his room, so I sought out Cam.

Chuck intercepted me on the way to Cam's suite and shook his head. "Cam's entertaining."

I rolled my eyes. Sure, sex was easy, and I'd jerked myself into nirvana enough to know orgasms felt good. But Cam, like my father, used sex to cover other pain.

"Let's head downstairs," Chuck said, probably watching the play of emotions across my face. "To the gym. You can punch the bag or run on the treadmill. Get rid of the pent-up emotion Aya brought out in you."

I reared back, away from the heavy hand on my shoulder. "Why does everyone think Aya's bad for me?"

Chuck resettled his large paw on my neck and steered me toward the elevator. "I like Aya just fine—better than I've liked any of the gals you boys bring around."

I crossed my arms over my chest and shot daggers into the silver elevator doors, making sure Chuck caught my look. "But?"

"But nothing." He shrugged.

"My dad fucks around instead of dealing with his grief about my brother. That's caused his marriage to fall apart." I frowned, knowing that wasn't quite right even as I said it. There had been women during the last tour, before Lev was gone. That's when Lev had pulled away from Dad, from me.

Chuck grunted. "And you're getting an altogether different lesson, aren't you, son?"

Steve, Cam, and Chuck all called me *son*, something my own father didn't. That realization left me unsettled.

When the doors opened, Chuck led me into the large gym and slid boxing gloves over my hands. "Punch it out if you don't want to talk any more."

I eyed the gloves, then him. "Is that what you do?"

He stuck his tongue between his teeth and considered. "Yeah. I got more of your lesson about sex and love. I prefer to pound my muscles into submission than screw my way to oblivion."

I tapped the gloves together and started hitting.

Definitely cathartic. Kendrick Lamar's lyrics pounded through my mind as sweat began to slide from my temples, then popped out over my whole body. I grunted and slammed my fists harder. I segued from straight-up rap to Beyonce's "Freedom," feeling totally jacked on the adrenaline high of boxing.

"All right, now. You're going to pay for that tomorrow." Chuck eased me back from the bag, tugging the gloves from my throbbing hands.

I looked at the clock and realized forty minutes had passed.

"Ready to talk about it?" he asked.

"I like Aya," I announced, stepping to the side.

"Shows you got taste." Chuck nodded. He tugged off his suit coat and rolled up his sleeves before he pulled on a pair of much larger gloves. He pounded at the punching bag, going harder than I thought possible.

Since he wasn't looking at me, I said, "Everyone calls her mine, and I even told her that's what I wanted, but I've seen what sex does to relationships. I don't think my parents like each other, let alone love one another, and—"

A firm hand slid onto my shoulder. I turned. Cam stared at me, a solemn look on his face.

"And you're worried about what that means for you and Aya," he said. He glanced at Chuck, seeming to make sure the bigger man was okay.

I didn't understand the bond between them, but I knew it was deep and important. Maybe like my connection with Cam…or with Steve.

"You guys and Steve are more like dads to me than my actual dad," I muttered. "I mean, here you are, keeping an eye on me.

You care what I'm thinking. My dad..." I swallowed, unsure how to voice my emotions about either of my parents.

Chuck quit swinging. He wasn't even out of breath. "You got good instincts," he said. He removed the gloves and grabbed his suitcoat. He walked over to the other side of the deserted space and grabbed a water from the fridge.

"You're all wound up about Aya—what she means to you and what she *should* mean to you," Cam said.

I continued staring at Chuck, but nodded.

"I met my wife when I was about your age."

I looked over, eyes wide.

"She's dead. Has been for a while." Cam waved his hand. "Story for another day, but it's part of why I don't like talking about my past."

I swallowed, digesting this new piece of information. "Fair enough."

He smiled. "Chuck's got his own story. One he prolly won't share. But it's why he's the way he is. Steve, too, I'm sure. Our choices before inform our decisions now—for better or worse. For a while now, mine have been for the worse."

I ingested his words, feeling their weight. "Can you come back from those decisions? Get on the right track?"

Cam scratched the side of his face, just above the dark scruff dusting his cheeks. I eyed it with a bit of envy. I shaved, sure, but I wasn't close to growing an actual beard.

"I don't rightly know. But I guess I should try, huh?"

Chuck came back and offered me a bottle of water. "Leaving the fan was a good start," he said to Cam.

Cam raised his eyebrow, his lips quirked in a sardonic grin. "She can't be worse than the crazy I lived through."

"Doesn't mean she's better."

"About Aya…" I said loudly.

Chuck tapped his fresh bottle of water against mine. "To pretty ladies with pure hearts."

I shook my head, not really understanding the comment. *Oh. Aya.* My eyes widened.

Cam laughed, turning me back toward the elevators. We rode down to the lobby, and when we exited, Chuck helped us ignore the crush of photographers and screaming women who begged for Cam's attention.

"Where are we going?"

"To grab a bite. I'm starving," Cam said.

I smiled. I was, too, and I liked getting out of the hotel. I also liked that Cam didn't fill his suite or floor with fans and partiers.

"What did you think about boxing?" Cam asked once we were settled in the vehicle.

"I like it."

"Chuck thought you might."

I smiled, feeling warmth in my chest. Cam liked me for me. I wasn't simply a tool to be used. He was like having a much older brother.

My chest ached. I'd always miss Lev, but Cam helped fill that gaping, ragged hole. And he seemed happy to do it. Just like Aya. She was a part of me—a deeper, more integral part, than Cam could be—which was why I wanted to share my successes with her. I remembered how good she felt in my arms, her soft hair tickling my skin, her fresh scent teasing my nose.

I'd already claimed a relationship with her. Now I had to make sure we could be close and not break apart, chip away at each other like my parents had.

"I'm definitely going to invite Aya to hang out again," I said. The decision was obvious now that my head was clear.

"All right," Cam said. "Just don't push for more'n you're ready to take on."

"Is that what you did?" I asked.

Chuck growled from the driver's seat, and Cam got a far-off look in his eyes. He pulled a candy from his ever-present stash and sighed a little when it hit his tongue.

"Oh yeah."

Chapter 17
Aya

As Nash appeared backstage with Cam at Madison Square Garden, my pulse raced and my mouth dried out. He wore his favorite red Chucks, dark wash jeans, and a soft gray T-shirt with an Austin logo I'd bought him for the occasion.

"*My good-luck shirt*," he'd said with a grin and a wink. "*From my pretty girl*."

He shoved his guitar back and pulled me into a tight embrace. His mouth sought mine, and I held still, one breath, two… His tongue caressed my lip, and I opened for him with a throaty gasp. I gripped his biceps, my head spinning. I whimpered as his tongue slid over mine in a long, slow swipe. I shivered, needing to be closer.

He pulled back, his hand on my chin, his gaze firm and filled with desire. "I could kiss you all night."

"After you kick ass on stage," I said.

He pressed a kiss to my temple. "Also for good luck," he murmured. Then he stepped back, leaving me shivering, missing his heat.

I huddled in my jacket, arms wrapped tight around my waist as he followed Cam toward the stage. My gaze slid down his broad back to the taut muscle under the soft denim. *Damn*, he looked good.

Nash settled into the spot next to Cam with an assurance that came from consistent rehearsals and performances since he'd left me in Boston a little over a month ago. In that time, his charisma had grown, and now he, like Cam, could carry the audience.

They started with "Sweet Baby Home," their harmonizing bringing tears to my eyes. After the song finished, Nash ribbed Cam about the intricacy of the guitar picking, even as he showed off his ability with an easy flourish that caused the crowd to hoot and holler in appreciation.

"Y'all wanna hear more from this guy?" Cam asked.

The crowd grumbled a little, but Nash picked and plucked his guitar faster as he hummed—that mesmerizing hum that made my knees weak and my body warm. He hummed a bit louder, the melody to the song he planned to play.

The crowd wavered, and the women began to holler and scream for more, more, *more*! Then Nash played in earnest. Cam stepped back, taking the rhythm-guitar role. When Nash leaned into the microphone, I would have sworn he'd been performing for years. He wasn't just a natural; he had an innate instinct for how to lift the crowd, how to create a fever pitch of emotion, and how to soothe them back into harmony. I pressed my clasped hands to my chest, tears pooling in my eyes.

Nash Porter, superstar, was born tonight, and I couldn't have been prouder. While I was the first one Nash hugged when he strode off stage, sweaty from the stage lights and clearly high on adrenaline, Steve was there, too, pulling him into a hard embrace. He thumped Nash on the back.

"Damn, you're someone a man can be proud of," Steve said, his voice wobbly.

Nash cast him a questioning look just as he was caught up by Chuck in a bone-crushing hug.

The night turned into a whirl of people congratulating Nash, of girls yelling his name, of reporters shoving closer to us as they called out questions, trying to scoop everyone else with the story of the new rock god—and get the real story behind Nash and Quantum's success.

Nash and I had talked about that over the past few weeks, and Nash had also spoken with Cam. Nash had chosen not to comment on his father or his father's band with the press, but Cam and some other stars, including Asher Smith, had questioned Brad Porter's composition skills—and whether he'd stolen his son's work.

Nash had blocked his father from his phone and social media, a bold but necessary step. While it made things more peaceful now, I wasn't sure what would happen when we returned to Austin—how Brad would handle the fallout from his ailing tour in combination with Nash's rising stardom. My guess was not well.

Nash handled his new fame with an ease I found disconcerting. Even now my skin itched, and I wanted to shrink away—except Nash had his arm around my shoulders, snuggling me against his side.

"Who's the girl?" a reporter yelled.

I cringed, and Nash looked down at me, his gleaming eyes dimming as he took in my uncertainty.

"Is that your girlfriend?"

"What's your name?"

"Smile for us, sweetheart."

"Why don't you give him a kiss?"

"Ignore them," Nash whispered.

I nodded, but unease crept through me because I knew the reporters would find their answers eventually—and I knew Nash's new fan base would work to tear me apart.

Chapter 18
Nash

My adrenaline high lasted through the rest of the evening, even as I tried to fully appreciate the iconic venue. Madison Square Garden—I'd just performed my own song here. *Holy hell.* Life was amazing. But the best part was Aya. She never left my side, and I liked her there. I held her hand on the way out of the building to the tour bus parked in the lot.

The song I'd shared tonight was a piece of me, one Aya held safe and close, inside herself. She understood the longing, the fear, the joy of whatever this was we were doing. And because she shared it, she made me feel brave enough to offer it out to the world.

Tonight I'd shared something, and it had proved magical, but I'd need to guard against the desire to offer up too much more. I could hear my mother's voice in my head. *No need to leave myself vulnerable.*

Cam had been saying he'd introduce me to Asher Smith for a while now, but our timing had always been off—until now. Reality hit hard as I watched him approach. I gripped Aya's hand, unable to slow my breathing.

She wiggled her fingers enough to return circulation and then leaned against me, her head on my shoulder, giving me the comfort I needed to calm down.

"You just faced down a crowd of how many thousand people?" she asked.

"They didn't matter. Not like this."

She sighed. "This is one on one, not all those fans you have to convince. *This* is easy."

Sure, easy for her to say. She wasn't supposed to have a *conversation* with Asher Smith. *The* Asher Smith. Oh, holy hell…the guy was on the bus, shaking hands with Cam and Chuck. I rose, tugging Aya up with me, unable or unwilling to let go of her hand.

Asher strode across the bus like he owned it—probably because he'd spent more of his life on one of these than I'd been alive. Like Cam, he wore black motorcycle boots. The shiny silver chains jangled with each step. His jeans were faded and worn—they looked comfortable, not designer. His pin-stripe button-up shirt was untucked, the sleeves rolled up to the elbows. His face was clean-shaven and his brown hair a tumble of waves—as if he'd been running his fingers through it, not using the product guys my age preferred. His intense eyes bored into mine, causing my palm in Aya's to sweat.

"Mr. Smith—"

"Asher," he said, a faint smile at the corner of his eyes and his mouth.

"A-Asher…" My tongue seemed to tie.

Aya stepped forward, her fingers gently squeezing mine. "I hear from Cam that your son likes to ride horses," she said with a smile. "My name is Aya Aldringham."

Asher shifted his focus to Aya, giving me a moment to breathe. "Mason does. He picked it up a few years back."

Aya began to recount a visit to a horse farm in Nepal, causing Asher to chuckle. "I'll have to bring Mason out to meet you tomorrow. He's about your age."

"That would be lovely," Aya said. "I'd love another friend to hang out with."

"Aya's the beauty and the charm of this duo," Cam said with a chuckle. "She's been a pleasure to have aboard, though she's been off at MIT doing some fancy robotics. But you gotta hear about her book choice, man." He turned to Aya. "Go on, tell him what you're reading."

Aya gauged my reaction before explaining her current historical fiction book choice to Asher freaking Smith. She was talking *book club* with the world's best lyricist.

Surreal.

He smiled at her, his white teeth gleaming. "Dahlia is going to love you." He leaned in closer to Aya, bending a little from the waist to make the moment more private between them. "My wife's an author. She got me into this Galileo series."

Aya gasped, eyes wide, as she named the book.

"That's the one."

"Oh, I'm desperate for the sequel, but it doesn't come out until next month."

"It's better than the first," Asher said, his tone confident.

"No way," Aya scoffed.

She *scoffed* at Asher Smith.

His eyes twinkled as he met my gaze and winked. He began to extoll the merits of the first book, causing Chuck to chime in. Seemed like they'd all read it but me.

And just like that, my tension eased. It wasn't gone—it shimmered over my shoulders and into my neck—but I could think again. I owed Aya, big time, for not letting me embarrass myself in front of my hero.

Asher seemed aware of my return to functioning status because he turned toward me when the book debate finally subsided. "Are you interested in signing with a label?" he asked.

I blinked at him, shock rocketing through me. I'd hoped for this, of course. But the reality—and with Asher as my mentor…

"If you are, I'd like you to consider my company," he continued. "We're based out of Seattle, which could be tricky since you're in Austin, but I think we can work something out."

My shock turned into bubbles of euphoria. Much as I wanted to tell him *hell yes* right here, I understood enough of the business to know one of my parents needed to sign off on the agreement. And it wouldn't be my father. "I need to discuss that with my parents."

Steve stepped forward, nervous but firm. "I can say that your parents will support this decision." His gaze met mine, softening in a way that caused my pulse to ratchet up. "If that's something you want."

I swallowed thickly, my hand trembling in Aya's.

"I don't have a band or…"

Asher nodded. "That's something I can help you with."

Asher will help me choose my bandmates? I felt lightheaded.

"Take the night. Talk it over with Cam, your folks. And don't make the decision lightly," Asher said. "Touring can eat you up." His gaze darkened. "It's why I like to stick close to my home base these days. I'm not all that interested in living on a bus and in a bubble of my bandmates, roadies, and staff." His eyes fell to where I gripped Aya's hand, and his gaze softened. "It's also damn near impossible to keep normal relationships. They suffer."

A chill swept over me as I inched closer to Aya.

With that, Asher turned back to Cam, asking him about a guitar maker in Austin. J. Olsen crafted them in a shop off of Sixth Street. Cam knew the maker, and he, Chuck, and Asher moved forward in the bus, leaving Aya and me in the back.

"Did that just happen?" I asked.

She smiled, the brightness seeming almost brittle, and her eyes shining, even in the low lights. "You're going to reach your every goal, Superstar."

I realized later that Aya had understood what Asher said and what it meant for us. Just as she understood that, despite all of that, I was desperate to take his offer.

Chapter 19
Aya

All that night, Nash vibrated with excitement, unable to sleep, pacing the suite's living room, on the phone with his mother and grandfather. We were at one of the Syads' hotel properties, and Nash had given Cam the penthouse, so we were a floor below, in a gorgeous suite with three bedrooms. It must have been five times larger than the average Manhattan apartment, with a mix of modern, geometric rugs and antique furniture. I fell asleep on one of the sofas, but I woke in my bed the next morning, a blanket tossed over me.

After using the bathroom and brushing my teeth, I changed into a clean outfit. Then I opened the door, and Nash practically accosted me.

"I signed the contract," he said, eyes burning with excitement.

"Oh! Well, great." I smiled as I wrapped my arms around myself, wishing his excitement would coat my worries.

"I had to tell you. I can't believe this is real, Ay. I can't…" He trailed off, his eyes wide, the dark circles under them telling.

I touched his cheek. "You need to get some rest before the show tonight," I murmured as I led him toward his bedroom. He followed, and now that he'd told me his news, the last of the adrenaline seemed to evaporate, leaving him exhausted. He settled on the bed, and I tugged off his sneakers.

"This is amazing," he mumbled. He rubbed his cheek against the pillow. "I'm going to write the perfect song…"

I pulled the comforter across the bed, covering him. I brushed the hair back from his forehead, my heart throbbing with love as his lashes fluttered.

Steve's comment to me the night before swirled through my head: *"He's going places you're not going to want to follow."*

That seemed abundantly true, especially considering Nash had been on stage, enjoying the adulation of the crowd, when Steve said it. Nash craved the spotlight while I wanted to sit in a cozy chair and read a book.

A few hours later, Nash knocked on my bedroom door. He poked his head inside. "Hey, can we talk?"

I closed my book and sat up, tucking hair behind my ear. Inwardly, I groaned. I was in a pair of black leggings and an oversized sweatshirt atop my sleeping camisole. Nothing about the outfit was sexy. I'd wanted to feel comfortable as I settled into the self-pity building in my head.

Tomorrow, I would go back to the last two weeks of my program. Nash would continue to tour, but I'd promised to visit him on the weekends as he and Cam worked their way up the East Coast.

He closed the door behind him, and I thought I heard him lock it.

"What's going on?" I asked. "Where is everyone?"

He tensed for a moment. "Steve's talking to my mom. Again. You know how long those calls go. And Chuck and Cam went to meet up with a friend."

So, we basically had the large, connecting suite to ourselves. A shiver slid down my spine as I considered my options. But then I shut down my hope that Nash would kiss me. He needed a friend—was desperate for the connection—and I'd promised myself I would be that for him. Even if it hurt.

Especially because it hurt.

"You don't seem excited about my record deal." He settled his hip next to mine on the bed.

It was a cushy mattress, and we rolled closer, separated only by the comforter and our pants. Need curled in my belly.

I forced the smile he needed. "Oh, I am." I rolled my eyes. "I'll get to tell people I was there for the birth of Nash Porter, Superstar."

His smile turned shy. "You really think I can be that? A superstar? Like Cam and Asher?"

I reached up and touched his cheek, letting my fingers linger. "I think you're going to blow them all away."

He studied me, no doubt looking for any insincerity. But he found none. I'd known, even as a small child, that Nash was destined for that stardom he'd mentioned. He practically shimmered with talent and possibilities. The fact that I'd held his interest this long was a gift.

"One of Asher's stipulations was that I had to finish high school before I record my album."

My belly warmed, and I smiled. Asher Smith cared about the musicians he worked with. Postponing Nash's album was a blessing, all the more so because Nash wanted to push forward so badly. This gave us time.

Nash leaned in closer—so close our noses nearly bumped. "I know you're upset about the girls flirting with me. But they don't matter."

I traced a pattern in the comforter next to my hip. "I'm sure one of them will be more than willing to keep you company once I'm gone."

"I want..." He blew out a breath. "I want you, Aya. To be with you."

Happiness exploded in my chest as I leaped forward in a tangle of limbs and sheets and tackled him to the bed. He laughed, his face so young and carefree, as he tucked my long hair back.

"You're everything to me," he said, his tone solemn. "If you weren't, I wouldn't be here right now. Maybe I should have pushed you away. But I couldn't. I can't."

I dropped my gaze.

He tipped my chin up, connecting us again. His gaze ignited nerve endings and sizzled down my spine, warming my belly.

"You've made me re-evaluate a lot of things, but mostly my stance on relationships. I kind of blindsided you at MIT, but I'm glad you went along with it—that you've stuck with me."

"Nash," I said on a sigh. "You have no idea what a beautiful guy you are. I'd choose you every time. I only want you."

His smile blinded me. "Good. Because I want to be with someone who makes my pulse race, who makes me forget where I am when I'm kissing her. Who makes me smile as soon as I think about her." His whiskey-brown eyes implored me. "That's you."

“I feel the same way,” I whispered. I leaned in a little, needing to feel his lips on mine.

He obliged, and they were warm, soft, as perfect as they’d been at that day under the oak trees. Except this time, he opened his mouth and tugged my hips even tighter to his. I slid my fingers into his hair and cupped his head, desperate to be as close to him as possible. I whimpered as need shot through me, causing my body to throb and feel hollow.

Our kisses morphed into hot, deep dances of tongue and teeth. He drugged me with pleasure, causing me to shiver and ache. His hand slid under my shirt, creeping to my chest, cupping my breast. I moaned into his mouth as he rubbed his thumb across my nipple.

“Your tits are my favorite thing,” he groaned against my mouth. “I need to see them.”

But he waited for me to reply. His face remained taut, his eyes luminous. Those luscious lips plumper than usual—because of passion, from wanting me.

“Yes, Nash. I want you to touch me.” *I want you to love me like I love you. That’s all I’ve ever wanted.*

But I bit those final words off, unwilling to say anything that might cause him to stop. Passion and foreboding drove me. I wasn’t sure what, exactly, this moment might become. Nash’s focus remained on my body, pushing away the pain of his reality. I wanted to keep him safe, in my arms, forever.

He buried his face in the valley between my breasts and held my back, his palms cupping my shoulder blades. His shoulders started to shake, but before I could offer comfort, he whipped up and took my lips in a punishing, drugging kiss.

His tongue penetrated my mouth even as his fingertips slid down my belly to the waistband of my leggings. He stripped me of those and my thong as he kneaded the supple flesh of my buttocks, pressing tiny kisses down my neck.

"Ay. God. *Aya*. You feel so good."

I panted, trying to catch my breath. He laid me back on the bed before he yanked his shirt over his head. When the warmth of his chest settled over mine, I gasped, arching into him, into the feeling of rightness pervading the moment.

"Feel me, Ay. Hold me, touch me." He nuzzled his nose against my ear.

Did he just ask me to love him?

Before I managed to process the words, his mouth covered mine again, his tongue tangling, dancing, dueling, leading mine.

"I want you," he said. He pulled back enough to meet my eyes. The storms that lived there were tempered by his desire. For me.

I slid my palm over his cheek. "I'm always here for you, Nash. Whatever you need."

"You," he whispered, pressing closer. "I need you."

I smiled. "You already have me."

"I want to have sex. With you," he clarified.

I leaned back on my elbows, spreading my thighs wide enough that he could see my wet folds. "I want that too. Very much."

He stood quickly so he could shuck his pants. His cock bobbed against his belly, the tip red and swollen, weeping. His sac nestled in brown curls that led to toned thighs and up to his taut abdomen. God, he was gorgeous.

He grabbed his wallet and pulled out a condom. I didn't have to ask why he had one—his father had handed him a box the first night of the tour.

Nash wanted me. And I wanted him—yes, physically, but just as much, I wanted his words, his heart, the happiness in his eyes. So I spread my legs, my heart pounding.

This was it. Nash and I were going to do this. Be together.

He opened the foil packet and rolled the condom on, the tip of his tongue pressing through his teeth as he concentrated. He settled at my side, his fingers finding my center, his thumb rubbing gentle circles over my clit.

"I want to make this good for you," he said.

I placed my hand on his cheek, loving the feel of his skin against mine. "And I want it to be good for you."

He smiled, no doubt liking my breathy voice. "It will be because it's you, Aya."

My heart melted and pounded all at once. This boy—how he made me feel.

He kept up his gentle ministrations until my thighs tensed and my body bowed. The orgasm hit me hard, leaving me breathless.

He kissed me softly, his gaze never leaving my face. "Good?"

I nodded, suddenly shy. Nash rolled over, settling between my thighs, nudging at my slick center.

"You okay with this?" he asked.

I tugged him closer, my arms wrapped tightly around his back. "Yes."

He was my love. I would never consider sex with anyone but Nash.

He was careful, watchful, as he pushed himself into my body. I bit my lip at the pinch of discomfort, but it passed as he bent his head to kiss me again. He thrust his tongue into my mouth as he pressed his cock into my body. I loved both. I loved being filled with him. I bucked my hips, wanting more. He pulled back, then pressed in.

"Oh…"

At my soft moan, he flexed his hips again, hitting a spot inside me that caused my nerve endings to blossom with pleasure.

I gripped the back of his head as I leaned up and kissed him. He caught a rhythm on the next stroke and pumped in and out. I spiraled up, seeking that pinnacle, striving for that beautiful release. His hips bucked as he cried out my name, and then he sagged against me. I lay still, breathing hard. After a moment, he pressed forward, into me again, and I arched against him.

He kissed my neck as he rubbed my clit with small, tight circles, sending more pleasure bursting through me. I cried out, quaking as those beautiful spasms built in my belly and cascaded through my limbs, leaving me limp.

After he'd dealt with the condom, he snuggled me close, his arm around my waist, my cheek on his chest.

"We're going to make this work, Aya. I know it. Because I need you as much as I need the music."

Even then, I knew he was lying—to himself and to me. But that didn't stop me from snuggling closer to his chest and holding on to him with all my strength.

Chapter 20
Nash

I glanced up at the small sound, pulling off my headphones, a smile growing as Aya stood in the open doorway to my hotel room. I'd been unable to pick her up from her summer camp, so I hadn't known when, exactly, I'd get to see her.

I rushed forward and pulled her into my arms. "I thought you were going to call me when you were home from your program."

She wrapped her arms around me. "I missed you too much to wait another day."

"Welcome to Denver," I said with a laugh.

She smiled. "Have you seen anything other than the hotel room?"

"Nope." I rolled my eyes. "Tour life."

She nuzzled into my chest, where happy bubbles exploded. I settled my hand at the base of her neck, fingers tangled in her thick hair. She tipped her head back, and I lowered my mouth. I'd missed kissing Aya. The soft brush of her mouth against mine, her subtle shift closer, the parting of her lips as she opened for me—I'd experienced it before, but electricity still jolted down my spine and more fizziness blossomed in my chest.

I delved in deeper, needing her. She tilted her head, granting me more access.

"Well, I guess you two are glad to see each other." Cam's amused voice drifted across the room.

I lifted my head, arms still wrapped around my girl. "Yeah. I'm ecstatic."

He smiled, wider and brighter than I'd seen before. "Good. Glad to have you back with us, Aya. And Steve will be here in ten minutes."

Cam winked before ambling off.

"Cam knew you were coming," I said, shuffling back enough so I could see her face.

She nodded. "I wanted it to be a surprise."

"The best."

She rose on her tiptoes and kissed me again. I moaned as her tongue brushed against mine. I yanked my head back and stared down at her, breathing hard. "Steve'll be here soon." That sounded more like a groan than words, but I didn't want to stop.

I also wouldn't embarrass Aya. No way would I have Steve see any part of her beautiful, sleek body, but I needed her naked. I needed to be inside her.

Her cool fingers touched my cheek, slipped down to the corner of my mouth. They trembled slightly, so I turned and kissed them.

"Maybe I shouldn't have come."

"You most definitely should have."

"But now we're both…" She blushed but held my gaze.

I leaned forward, inhaling her soft scent. "I'm going to get you alone, to myself, soon," I murmured before I nipped her ear. She yelped just as the suite door slammed shut.

"Hey, Nash, Cam said he wants to leave for the stadium in an hour." Steve stopped in the doorway. He smiled as he took in

Aya. I did, too. She wore a long sundress that left her shoulders bare. Low-heeled sandals showed off her bright green toenails. They matched the leaves in her floral-print dress. Her long hair was loose, waving over her shoulders and down her back.

Her makeup was light, soft, natural, and most of her lip gloss had rubbed off—on my mouth no doubt. I smiled, satisfaction blooming at the plump pinkness of her lips. She was so beautiful.

"Good to see you, Aya. How was MIT?"

A faint shudder rippled down from her shoulders. "Okay. I'm glad to be finished."

Steve nodded.

I grabbed her hand and tugged her toward my bed. "Why just okay? What didn't you tell me? Was that girl mean again?"

"We're leaving in an hour," Steve reminded me. "Want something sent up before we have to go?"

I looked at Aya, who shook her head. There'd be plenty to eat at the stadium, all part of the standard contract, so I shook my head, too.

"Tell me everything," I said.

She dropped her gaze to her hands, which were now clasped in her lap. "I missed you, " she blurted.

"I missed you, too," I said. I lay down on the unmade bed and pulled her to my chest. She snuggled close.

"No, I mean I really missed you. And, yeah, Li was a problem, but I dealt with it."

She caught me up on the camp, and I filled her in on our more recent shows. "I've been trying to write a few songs for the album Asher wants me to make."

She drew patterns on my chest, causing goose bumps to ripple over my arms and my nipples to tighten. Fuck. This girl owned my body.

"How's that going?" she asked.

I grunted. She lifted her head and stacked her palms, resting her chin on them. Her violet eyes held mine. "Your songs give me chills. I've seen you perform. I have no doubt that you're going to make something amazing."

I swallowed the lump in my throat, unable to tell her how much those words meant to me.

As I performed that night, knowing Aya stood in the wings amped me up. Each show that week was better than the last. I loved looking over and seeing her there.

But I was glad when we returned to Austin the following week. Eight weeks of new cities, the late nights, all of it had caught up with me, and I planned to crash hard when we arrived at Cam's ranch. And Monday was the first day of school. Jeez. Might have cut that a little close…

Cam invited Aya and me to stay the night with him, but she politely declined, explaining that she wanted to see her mother. Mama Grace insisted on feeding us before she allowed Steve to drive us back to Aya's house, but once he did, Mrs. Didri-Aldringham met us at the door. The smell of chai, butter, and sugar wafted from the kitchen as she hugged us both.

"Mrs. Ombly and I made Madeleines," Mrs. Didri-Aldringham said, her hand smoothing back Aya's hair. Her smile was blinding, but her face was thinner, paler than I remembered. Her eyes were bright with happiness. "They're Aya's favorite."

I nodded. "I remember. I like them, too."

She smiled and went to get us both mugs of tea and a plateful of cookies. I wanted to stay there, in that kitchen, for the rest of the night—mainly because I dreaded going home. Steve had told me earlier that my dad was there and in a foul mood. I hadn't asked for details because I'd read enough of the press to know critics continued to pan his album and the band had canceled the second half of their tour.

As we nibbled, we caught Aya's mom up on the tour. She already knew about my record deal.

"Mrs. Ombly and I made up the guestrooms," Mrs. Didri-Aldringham said, "in case you wanted to stay here tonight. I know you have to collect your school items before class on Monday. I can't believe it's the first day of your senior year."

I reached under the table and squeezed Aya's hand.

"Thanks, Mom," she said, smiling. "We've spent so much time together that it's going to be weird not seeing Nash all the time. And now we can all have breakfast together before Nash and I hit the mall." She beamed at me, and I realized she'd set this up. She knew I would have stayed at the ranch to buy more time away from my father. Gratitude filled me.

Mrs. Didri-Aldringham smiled, her thumb brushing a crumb from Aya's cheek before she cradled it in her palm. "Mind if I tag along? I've missed seeing you."

"I'd like that," I said.

I couldn't remember the last time my mother took me shopping. She sent me gifts, often, and she called, but I wasn't sure the last time I actually saw her. I hated that she preferred to live in Europe than with me, but I wasn't willing to leave Aya or Cam—even though I craved the closeness Mom and I had once had.

I smiled as I looked over at Aya. The next year spread out before me, like a movie, and I liked what I saw. Asher had insisted I take this year, my senior year, as part of the deal—he wouldn't let me begin recording until next summer. That meant I had nine months with Aya. Our classmates would find out about my touring with Cam and my record deal, and that would keep me at the top of our social hierarchy—not that I cared that much.

Sure, we'd have schoolwork, and I'd write a million terrible tunes with only a few that were good enough to show Asher next summer, but I also knew I'd spend hours in this kitchen, in this house, in Aya.

"Thanks," I murmured. I wiped my fingers on a napkin and tucked some of Aya's hair behind her ear.

She nuzzled into my hand, her eyes bright and filled with so much emotion. "Anything to make you happy."

Contentment washed over me. For the first time in years, I *was* happy.

Chapter 21

NINE MONTHS LATER

Aya

Loving Nash was easy, like breathing. No, easier. I'd done it for so long, unknowingly, that it was simply a part of who I was. However, the reality of being his girlfriend and attending Holyoke was more complicated. Every once in a while these days, I'd get a call from a reporter who wanted a story on Nash, Asher Smith's newest star. I always declined to comment, jealously guarding his secrets. But the girls at school had been another matter.

They'd fawned, they'd rubbed against Nash while sliding their phone numbers into his pocket, and they'd talked about me. I was aware of the online groups where girls discussed the many ways I wasn't pretty or sexy enough to date Nash. They made fun of my college goals, wondering why I would bother with an education when I could simply tour with him. They debated why he wanted to have sex with me.

It felt awful to know that was out there, but I had done my best to ignore those comments, blatant or insidious, and just focus on my life, on Nash. We'd spent every lunch together, and he'd often come to my house after school. The situation with his father had nose-dived, and while Nash didn't speak of it much, each time he went home, he returned quieter.

Mum had agreed that Nash's home life wasn't the best, so she never questioned him staying over. Steve often stayed with us, too, which my mother seemed to enjoy. She beamed over the dining table, pleased to have it filled.

During our senior year, Nash and I went to homecoming, to the Valentine's dance, and to prom. My mother and Steve took tons of pictures before each, and I'd framed my favorites, setting them on a shelf in my room next to my bureau.

Nash had held me in his arms on more than one occasion as I worried over my mum's weight loss, which she always chalked up to exhaustion, though neither Nash nor I bought that story.

He'd asked her point-blank one night if she was sick.

She didn't answer.

But at least he'd asked. At least he'd tried.

When I looked back over the year, I guessed loving Nash had held me together with the weirdness that was both the perfect romance and occasionally a source of inner turmoil for me. But we had each other, we hung together, and that was all I could ask for. He was my safe place, my home.

However, while loving Nash came naturally to me, sometimes getting along with him was a whole other issue.

Like now. He was in a foul mood, brought about by his dad's sex-with-a-groupie video making the rounds on the internet. That press had his mother smiling impossibly wider, her eyes empty as she hit each of the clubs on Milan's strip, and even as she called Nash to tell him she'd sent divorce papers to Brad.

"I just can't anymore," she said.

I could hear her through his phone speaker, so I shifted away. But Nash pulled me down onto his lap, tucking my head under his chin as he leaned back into the pillows on my bed. I sought out my UT pennant on the opposite wall.

MIT hadn't accepted me, so I'd decided to stay here, close to my mother and Nash.

I couldn't wait to start classes at UT in August. Now that our high school graduation was behind us, Nash and I could focus on our goals: he would fly to Seattle June 1 to finish the album he'd started here, with Cam, at Asher's studio, and I'd spend the summer there with him.

We had an apartment near Pike Place already chosen. Part of me couldn't believe we were doing this. But I was giddy with excitement.

"Fine. I get it. He's a total douche," Nash said. I could hear the deep rumbles of his chest. I pressed my cheek against the soft cotton of his T-shirt. "But you're still coming back, right?"

She was supposed to be here, in Austin, for Nash's graduation party at Cam's family ranch next weekend. The end-of-May event had been planned for months.

"No, honey. I can't… I just can't face it. Face him." Tears lined her voice. "Please don't hate me," she sobbed. "I can't stand for you to hate me."

"I don't hate you, Mom." Nash sighed.

And he didn't, but that didn't mean he understood her choices—or liked them.

"You can come visit me," she said, perking up. "I'll meet you in Paris—"

"I have to finish my album."

He didn't add *remember?* to it this time. She didn't, probably because she was on too many substances to think much at all.

"Oh. Well. After, then. I can't wait to see you, Nash."

She sounded like a small child, unable or unwilling to be reasoned with.

"I'll be starting my tour after that," he said, his voice patient.

"Oh. Well, then…Christmas."

"Sure," he said. "I'll see you then. Bye, Mom."

He slammed the phone down onto my bed with enough force to cause us to bounce.

"What the fuck does she think she's doing?" he growled.

I slid off him, and he rose to prowl around my room.

Prior to last summer, Nash rarely came into my room, but my mother had grown too enamored with him during our almost year of dating to enforce the rules. This meant we did pretty much as we pleased. And we'd experimented. A lot. I flushed as I remembered last night.

"Stop thinking about sex," he snapped.

"I wasn't," I said, though we both knew I lied. I raised my gaze to his as I licked my lips. "Fine. I was. I really enjoyed last night."

The anger melted from his face. "Did you now?"

"Mmm... I'm glad you talked me into trying…that."

My face flushed as my gaze dropped to his jeans. The soft fabric cupped him like my hand, caressing the package there. My breath hitched. Oh, how I wanted him.

He loomed over me, his eyes stormy, but his lips soft, parted in invitation. I leaned forward and pressed mine against them.

He settled back on his heels, his hand at the nape of my neck, tugging me upward so my chest rested against his.

Eventually we came up for air, and Nash flopped onto my queen-size bed, looking out of place on the pale pink, ruched comforter. Yet, at the same time, his big, rangy body looked just right.

He'd turned eighteen nearly three months ago, and I'd had my birthday ten days after. He'd had Steve take us to the Hill Country, and then he'd surprised me by renting out one of my favorite restaurants. He'd invited my mother, Hugh, and Hugh's new girlfriend, Lindsay Herrington-Smythe.

Yes, that mean girl Lindsay. But Naomi had dumped Hugh, and he'd become enamored with Lindsay. And Hugh was my friend, so we'd included her in my celebration. I'd gritted my teeth each time Lindsay leered at Nash—nothing new, really, as most girls looked at Nash that way. But Lindsay's gaze held something more, a calculation and coldness. When she caught me looking, she'd smirk, and I'd shiver.

My mother hadn't attended. Her health had declined over the last few months, and each time I looked at her once-lively eyes—which seemed to sink deeper into her skull every night as she slept—I feared she wouldn't be with me much longer. And she wouldn't be able to keep her promise to limit my father's involvement in my life.

Her body wanted to give out, but her will remained strong. Unfortunately, I wasn't sure her will could win this battle.

Nash's flop of sun-kissed hair tangled with his eyelashes and his T-shirt had ridden up, giving me a glimpse of the warm, honey skin of his belly. He was taller now—over six feet—and he'd bulked up, especially during this past school year, thanks to the personal trainer he'd hired to teach him about boxing.

"Hugh is thinking about breaking up with Lindsay." Nash shifted on the bed, finding a more comfortable position. He tossed his phone to the side. "He says she's clingy."

I wrinkled my nose but didn't say anything.

"Maybe she'll end up back in England with her dear old dad," Nash mused. "She's miserable here, so that makes the most sense."

I shrugged. I knew Lindsay's father was British, like mine, and her mother had taken a position at one of the tech firms here, handling their PR. I also knew Lindsay wanted very much to have Nash for herself. That's why she'd started dating Hugh and wore her shortest skirts and figure-hugging jeans or halter tops.

I lay against his side, enjoying the warmth from his body.

"I'm going to miss you," I murmured, hating the idea of him going to Seattle before me.

My mother asked me to spend this next week with her, and I couldn't tell her no, nor had Nash wanted me to. He longed for that sort of closeness with his mother, but she'd become even more distant this past year. And that had made it difficult for me to like her. Her son needed her, and she preferred to pretend her life was one big party.

"And I don't like the idea of you being sad or angry at your parents," I added.

"I'll call you every day." He pulled me down onto the bed, and I sprawled over him, my dark hair a curtain that blocked out most of the light. "This is the first time we'll be apart since that tour with Cam." He tucked hair behind my ear.

I nodded. A lot of things were changing, coming to an end. While I was excited to travel to Seattle with him, I knew I would miss this time, this closeness. His record deal would change his life—and mine. I wondered what things would be like in a year... Nash needed to travel, to explore, to perform. I needed the stability of my mother, my home, which was why I'd opted out of the dorms. Too many pieces of my life were shifting because of Nash's growing fame.

This year, he'd been content to spend time with me, but with the move to Seattle, I doubted that would remain true.

"I know this is important," I told him. "You have your album to work on. You need to finish that and continue to build your audience."

He stared into my eyes, his grip becoming firmer, more electric. My breath quickened. He stared at me, hunger in his eyes. "I need *you* more."

Chapter 22
Nash

Just like every other time I'd been with Aya, this time had been *perfect.* Paul Simon crooned over his guitar, the riffs to "Kodachrome" drifting through my head.

"I love you," Aya whispered, completing the ritual I'd come to need. But then she did something different. She raised her head and met my gaze. "Do you love me, Nash?"

She tried to keep her face relaxed, but fear darkened those beautiful violet eyes as she searched mine. I did, of course, but as I opened my mouth, the words stuck in my throat. Memories I'd never shared with Aya rushed to consume me.

"*I love you, Carolina. Why can't you just leave it at that?*" Dad had growled at Mom.

Lev and I had huddled close, just inside the large glass wall, peering out onto the deck, straining to catch every word of their fight.

"*See?*" Lev had sneered. "*He uses the words, but he doesn't mean them.*"

I'd watched him swallow another handful of pills—this time brazenly, almost begging our parents to see him, stop him.

"*Because love shouldn't involve other women!*" Mom had shrieked back.

Dad had stood then, his phone falling from this lap to the

flagstones below.

Lev had grunted, reaching his limit. "*I'll show that stupid fucker*." He'd darted out toward Dad's phone. He'd grabbed it, shaking it over his head. I could still see his thin, pale arm stark against the black sky and his dark T-shirt.

"*Maybe if you turned off the notifications for your fuck buddies, Mom would believe you*," he'd taunted.

Dad had whirled, eyes and mouth wide before he lunged. Lev darted away, nimble despite the drugs that caused him to sway.

"*Choose*," Lev called, running down the stairs. "*Do you love Mom or do you love banging lots of women? Huh? What's it going to be, asshole*?"

I'd shoved open the door Lev had slammed behind him, screaming his name. Dad's anger had blurred the air around him as he snarled at Lev to give him back his phone. And then everything moved in slow motion…

Lev running to the end of the dock.

Lev throwing the phone.

Lev teetering.

Lev falling.

Lev gone.

"Nash?" Aya's cool hand settled on my cheek, tugging me back to the present. "It's okay," she said, her mouth trembling. "I shouldn't have pushed. I'm just glad you're here with me."

She kissed me, and I responded, desperate. Love was *stupid*, futile. *It hurt.* But this…what Aya and I had, it was *more* than love could ever be.

I just needed her to understand. But I tasted the saltiness of tears at the corners of her lips. Tears I'd made her cry.

"Are you going to find another girl on the tour?" she whispered.

I pulled back and settled her head against my chest. "I'm here with you. That's all that matters."

"Is it?" she asked.

"Yeah, it is." I held her, feeling like an asshole. Why couldn't I just say what she needed to hear?

But I couldn't get the words to come out. I just couldn't.

She sniffled for a while before she relaxed into sleep. I stared down at her, wishing I'd done a better job reassuring her tonight.

My phone beeped a text, then another and another.

I grabbed it, turning it to silent mode as I looked back at Aya. I sighed, my shoulders relaxing, as she slept on. I wanted to curl around her and sleep, too. It was late, and I was exhausted, but I couldn't relax. Not here, not after what I'd done to Aya—or hadn't done, actually.

Dried tear tracks had crusted white on her cheeks. I frowned, hovering there, wanting to do something to ease her concern, to explain. But how could I explain? Then I'd have to share the whole story, and I didn't want that. Didn't want to *think* about that.

My phone vibrated, then again and again.

With a curse, I pulled on my clothes and headed out her bedroom door.

I slammed through my front door, annoyance and fear jockeying for dominance after the sheer number of texts my father had sent me. I felt keyed up and restless until the moment I found my father face down in his own vomit in the marble-tiled atrium. Then everything in me went still.

"Dad!"

My knees slammed to the ground, and I gritted my teeth against the pain as I rolled him to his side. He let out a low moan.

He isn't dead. I couldn't lose someone else.

He met my gaze, and tears filled his bloodshot eyes.

"She's leaving me," he murmured. His voice cracked. "Carolina…she's really *leaving me.*"

He screamed the last so loudly that I fell on my ass, right in a puddle of my father's sick.

He curled up in a fetal position and sobbed. "I loved her," he rasped, his voice shredded. Then he sprung up and gripped my shirt, his eyes wild, tears streaming down his face. "You gotta believe me. I loved her so much. I never wanted this—I never wanted her to leave me."

I stared, unsure what to do, how to manage this crazed version of my father.

Then Steve hauled me off the floor.

"What's happening?" I asked. Confusion pummeled me, but Steve was a steadying presence. Yet even as I was grateful for him, my mother's long-held insistence on discretion and privacy told me Steve shouldn't witness this. Still, I clutched his sleeve as I stared at my father's huddled form.

"He's not supposed to be here."

"What?"

With a look of disgust, Steve said, "He's clearly having some kind of a breakdown."

"Is my mom…?" I felt like a little boy again, begging for attention. Please, please let her just be hurt. We could survive hurt.

Steve shook his head. "Your mom's fine. She's still in Paris. Brad here just received his divorce papers."

"As in today?"

Steve nodded. "Why don't you go on upstairs and get in the shower? I'll do my best to get him cleaned up." His lip curled in disgust as he bent down to haul my dad off the floor. "And get him out of here."

"No," I said. I licked my lower lip. "I need to talk to him."

Steve narrowed his eyes. "I don't think that's a good idea, Nash."

I straightened my spine and met my bodyguard's gaze. "I didn't ask."

Steve's jaw ticked, but he dipped his head once. I hoped that meant he agreed.

I made it into my shower on autopilot and stood there, hot water pounding against my skin and "Carry on My Wayward Son" pounding through my brain.

My dad was a disaster.

But nothing about this situation made sense. He had to know Mom would eventually reach her breaking point. How could he not know that?

I scrubbed my face. I wished I hadn't come home. If only I'd stayed in Aya's bed. We'd been happy. My chest ached. No, we hadn't. I'd hurt her. I'd need to figure out how to fix that, too.

After a good, long soak that did very little to make me feel any cleaner, I dressed and tried to pull myself together in my room. Still, I hesitated before heading back downstairs. I considered calling Pop Syad, but I wasn't sure he was in good enough health to help me. And what would I ask him to do from Paris, anyway?

But there was something about finding my dad tonight, how unhinged he'd become… Fear crept up the back of my neck, and I struggled against the need to run.

I needed to man up and deal with my father, so I strode down the stairs toward the master suite, my heart pounding so hard against my ribs that it drowned out any possibility of music in my head.

Dad looked up at me as I stepped into his room, his eyes bloodshot, red-rimmed, and empty. At least he was clean now, his hair wet from his recent shower.

"I need some answers," I said.

He turned to look out the window. When he turned back, his gaze locked on mine. "You think I'm to blame for all this. I know you do."

I heard a gentle clearing of a throat and turned to see Steve on the other side of the room, near the door, like he couldn't bring himself to get any closer. His mouth pressed in a thin, disapproving line.

"What?" Dad snapped. "Carolina's father is going to shove me out on my ass anyway—we both know it. At least Nash deserves the truth."

"Don't—"

"Fuck off, Steve. This is as much your fault as it is mine." Dad had tried to yell that, but his vocal cords seemed too shredded to get out more than a hoarse croak. He wheeled back to face me. "You aren't my son."

"Wha…?" Of course I was. We shared a love of music, the same color hair…and nothing else.

"Brad—" Steve moved farther into the room, his agitation clear.

"Blow me," Dad replied. "You cuckolding bastard." His gaze turned malicious. "Didn't he tell you? Steve is part of the long list of boy-toys your mother screwed. Him showing up here was how I figured it all out."

I couldn't think. My head spun around like a top.

Brad choked out a laugh. "Ironic, huh? I'm the one known for my affairs when *Carolina* destroyed our marriage."

"You were," I yelled. "I saw you with—with all those women."

Brad grinned, flashing those white, perfect teeth, but his eyes were dark, dank—deep pits of the ugly he'd lived. "To get even with Carolina," he said as if it were the most rational thing in the world. "To make her feel the jealousy I did. It worked for a while, but after Lev died…"

He tugged at his hair, and pieces of it came away in his fingers. That horrified me as much as his words. Brad Porter was coming apart right in front of me. Fear slicked my insides, and my skin crawled.

"I'm going to have to ask you to leave the premises," Steve said, coming forward to tower over Brad. He refused to meet my seeking gaze.

"What's he talking about?" I asked. My voice sounded high, thin—that of a child. "Steve, why did he say that about my mom?"

"Get up, Bradley," Steve said, his tone hard. "You broke the contract with malice. You have to leave the premises right now."

"What?" I cried. "Wait! You can't just kick my dad—"

"I'm not your father, you stupid shit," Brad growled, standing up. "Didn't you hear me? You mother's a—"

I lunged at him, gripping his shirt, and he laughed.

"You gonna take a swing at me, you pathetic little punk? Fine. *Hit me*. I'll get more out of you for assault than I would from my control-freak father-in-law." He shook himself loose from me. "Here's a news flash: I never wanted another kid. Lev was more than enough for me. I loved him. You...you were good at writing music. That's *all*. That's the only reason I pretended to like you. But then you had to go and tell Carolina's fuck-toy here all about it, ruining the one thing we could have had."

Steve didn't have to pull me away from Brad. I stepped back all on my own, shaking my head, my mouth hanging open, my world caving in on itself.

Brad laughed again, and I shivered, hating the way the sound accosted my ears. It was discordant, vicious.

Steve dragged Brad from the room, a meaty arm over his chest as he kicked.

I couldn't see Steve's face, but his shoulders were stiff.

Alone in the room, I saw black creeping in around the edges of my vision. My eyes burned and my head ached. I'd just collapsed in a chair when Steve returned, his phone in hand.

"Your grandfather would like to speak to you."

I shook my head. "Just tell me... Is it true? What my da—what Brad said? Was that true? Did you have an affair with my mom?"

Steve's face remained stoic, but his eyes gave him away. They were dark, filled with secrets. He held out the phone again. "You should really talk to your grandfather."

"I asked you a question," I said.

His jaw jutted forward. "Nash, it's not that simple…"

I stepped back, my guts churning, my mind whirling. "That's the thing. It is. You let this happen to me. *You went along with it.*"

"Nash." His voice cracked. I'd never seen Steve lose his composure. But now his jaw trembled.

"No. I don't want to talk to anyone. You've all lied to me." I stabbed my finger toward Steve's face. His eyes dimmed further. "You lied to me," I screamed. "All of you. And my mom…" A sob erupted as I ran from the room, tore out the front door.

I'd go to Aya. She'd know what to do.

I ran, picking up the pace, ignoring the gravel and detritus that cut into my feet.

I needed this night to never have happened. I'd go back to Aya's house, to her bed, and wrap myself around her.

I'd wake up in the morning, and this would all be a dream.

A terrible, terrible nightmare.

Chapter 23
Aya

Sometime in the night I rolled over, and my hand settled on the cool sheet next to me. I sat up, my stomach roiling. "Nash?"

The room was dark and cool. Quiet. Too quiet for Nash to still be there—he snored, though he didn't believe me when I said so. As I pulled the sheet up over my naked chest, the faint sound of something shifted across the linen. With a squeak, I dove for the nightstand light and flicked it on as I jumped from the bed. I darted across the room and shimmied into a nightshirt and panties before creeping back toward the mattress.

I sighed, relief making my limbs limp when I saw the folded piece of paper with my name on top. I rubbed my thumb over Nash's messy scrawl. My chest tightened as I unfolded the paper with extra care.

I didn't want to leave. My dad kept texting, asking where I was. If I could have stayed, I would have. I wanted to wake up next to you. I wanted to kiss you again. I always want to kiss you. I'll never get enough of your time or kisses.

Yours,

Nash

I traced my fingers over the letters. See? He *must* love me; he just struggled with the words. And who could blame him? His parents were a hot bloody mess. He just needed more time. He'd tell me eventually.

Someone knocked on my door as I frowned at the paper, wishing the *Yours* said *Love*. He didn't have to *say* the words for me to know how he felt…

"I'm sorry to bother you, Miss Aya, but we need to take your mother to the hospital."

I set Nash's paper on my nightstand. "What's wrong?" I asked.

"Get dressed. I've called the ambulance as I think that's better than me transporting her."

I chewed on my lip as I pulled on a pair of leggings and a long tunic. I hurried down the hall, my head spinning, and burst into my mother's room. It was light, airy, with sheer curtains at the large windows that overlooked the lake. Her large, balsawood bed had the sheers tied back. She lay huddled in the middle of them.

"Mum," I cried, rushing toward her.

"Didn't want to worry you, mon mignon," Mum said, gasping and wheezing.

She seemed to shrink before my eyes. The wheezing grew louder. Her hand was cold, her fingers like frail, brittle twigs between my palms.

"You'll be fine," I said with a smile. "Everything will be fine. I love you."

"Ah, ma petite belle. I love you too—to the moon and back again."

"What is it? I asked.

"Heart…chest pains…" She began to cough, hacking grunts that shook her frame.

My whole body shook—maybe from the shock, I wasn't sure. I'd been sitting here, in this spot, mere hours before, and my mother was fine. She'd laughed with me.

Moments later, the housekeeper, Mrs. Ombly, pushed open the solid pine door, admitting paramedics. I was shunted to the side as they spoke in their medical shorthand.

Mrs. Ombly drove me to the hospital. I sat at my mother's bedside in the ICU. My mother's nurse had disappeared some time ago, her face haggard, after saying she couldn't do anything more.

Mrs. Ombly suggested I call my father, and that's when I realized I didn't have my phone. She promised to collect it and a change of clothes for me. I must have fallen asleep after she left, because the next time I woke, the machines were screaming and people rushed into the room, moving me out.

I waited in the hall outside my mother's room as more medical personnel sprinted inside. But I didn't need them to tell me what I'd seen in my mother's eyes.

Chapter 24
Nash

Aya still hadn't responded to my messages, which was unlike her. And she hadn't been home when I'd run here. Dark, clamorous instruments clashed in my head—a heavy, angry hiss of noise that flared with fear and worry.

The house was open, though, so I'd come in to wait for her. That's when I found her phone in her room. I'd laid down on her bed and stared up at the ceiling, inhaling her scent. It had calmed me, and I'd sighed just before the sob caught me by surprise. Then I turned my head into her pillow and cried. *My dad—Brad… He hated me.*

All the while my phone had kept buzzing in my pocket. I ignored it as long as I could, but finally, I yanked it out in irritation. Pop Syad had called me fifty-three times.

He called me a fifty-fourth while I was checking, so I pressed the green button.

"What?" I snapped.

"I'm worried about you, my boy."

"I'm fine."

"No, Nash, you're not. And it's because of that…that…"

I rose from Aya's bed and moved toward her dresser. My eyes traveled over her phone and the note I'd written her next to it, and then found her malas. My fingers wrapped around the beads, and I ran my thumb over the tassel, enjoying the tickling sensation across my skin. She'd taken them off to shower earlier, I remembered. She didn't like the tassel to get wet.

Where is she? I should go check on her mother, make sure everything's okay.

I shoved my hand into my pocket and moved back across Aya's room.

"Your mother is a beautiful woman," Pop Syad added after a moment. "So vivacious and full of life. But she needed a firm hand. Rules. Brad broke all the rules. He broke her."

I headed toward Mrs. Didri-Aldringham's room.

"Steve is in front of the Didri estate. Please join him, Nash. There is much I need to tell you."

I huffed out a breath. "I don't want to see him. Or you. I don't want to talk to either of you."

"Brad Porter is in debt," Pop Syad said quickly, pressing into the silence before I managed to turn off my phone. I put it back to my ear. "Large amounts of debt. That's why he took money from me to stay with you while your mother spent time during the last years in and out of various rehabilitation facilities." He sighed. "I feel as though I've tried every one in Europe."

I stopped walking, my mouth dropping open. "But her partying, I saw her…"

"I wanted to tell you, but she was ashamed. It's been a downward spiral. She'd finish treatment, and Brad would pull something terrible. I've been trying to get her to divorce him for years. Her health is *his* fault. Finally, she's seen reason. The only way to get well is to cut out the tumor."

"The women," I said, my tone flat.

"She's trying to get clean for you. She told me she made you a promise before her last trip. She promised to get clean and spend time with you."

"She failed."

"Alcoholism is a disease, Nash. One that needs to be monitored."

"It's not just alcohol, though, is it?" I asked.

He sighed. "No, it isn't. She struggles with all substances."

"And sex," I said, hating the words.

My head swam. I didn't know what to think, what to do. So much had changed. In less than a day, I'd learned sordid, terrible truths about my mother, lost my father… My grandfather's illness loomed large. This was how Aya felt every day, I realized—a sick fear that everything she understood and knew would soon be gone, that everything she wanted would be ripped from her.

"I need you to go with Steve, no matter your current anger with him," Pop Syad insisted.

"I don't want—"

"I know that. I know you're an adult. I know I can't force you to do anything. But you're also the heir to my fortune, and your parents just dropped one of the biggest stories to hit the media this decade. Their divorce is going to be a shitshow. Brad will make sure of it. So please, until this settles down, please stay with Steve."

I heard the door downstairs click open. If Mrs. Didri-Aldringham was sleeping, I didn't want to wake her.

"Fine, but I don't want to see you or my mother."

Not that I expected her to come home. Why now, after all this time? I needed to process this. Fuck, I needed Aya.

I didn't bother to say goodbye as I hung up and headed down the stairs toward Steve's hulking form. He latched his large paw around my biceps, letting me know I wasn't leaving his sight anytime soon.

Just fucking great.

Chapter 25
Aya

When Mrs. Ombly returned, she led me to the closest waiting room and wrapped my fingers around a Styrofoam cup of tea. I held it, staring at the ill-fitted tiles on the floor as I sank into a chair.

"Would you like your phone, Miss Aya? Maybe Nash could come sit with you."

"Sure," I murmured, my voice hoarse. My throat ached with unshed tears. I took the device from her, clicked on the screen, and gasped. The tea fell from my hand, splattering my sandals and foot with hot liquid. But I didn't feel it. Not then. Not as my gaze roamed over the many lines of text Nash had sent me—begging me to respond, saying he needed me.

I read all the way to the last one.

My father told me some serious shit. I really, really fucking need you right now.

But before I could reply, the doctor strode into the waiting room. I rose, slipping a little in the spilled tea. Mrs. Ombly bent down to clean it up with the thin tissues from the table.

"She had a massive heart attack," he said. "We had to go in for emergency bypass."

"Is she…" I couldn't form the word.

He scrubbed a hand through his messy hair. "She pulled

through the surgery, but it's going to be touch and go for a while. This was a major event. She's very sick."

"With what?" I asked.

Mrs. Ombly made a noise.

He frowned. "She didn't tell you?"

I shook my head.

He settled into the chair beside me. "Your mother has coronary artery disease."

"What does that mean?" I fiddled with my fingers. "That's why she…she had a heart attack?"

He nodded. "It's genetic. We don't understand why, but that connection can cause more serious health issues for women."

"My grandfather… That's why we moved back…"

Over the next few minutes, the doctor answered my halting questions, though I had a sinking feeling I didn't know enough to figure out what to ask, what to even hope for. My mind whirled after he rose. He patted my shoulder once and strode away.

Mrs. Ombly placed her hand on my knee. "She didn't want to worry you."

My eyes were dry. My body numb. My jaw trembled as I raised my phone and typed out the necessary words to Nash: *My mom's in the ICU.*

Chapter 26
Nash

Showing up at Hugh's birthday party the next evening was a stupid idea, but I didn't know where else to go. He'd invited me weeks ago, before my world fell apart, and I'd already RSVPed—at least that's what I told Steve.

I glowered around the room, annoyed by its clean lines and low-backed, white leather couches. This was Hugh's father's place, and he'd had it all done up in mid-century modern after he divorced Hugh's mom a few years back. She'd hated the minimalist lines, Hugh said, which made it appeal to Dr. Peckham all the more.

Fifty or so kids—the boys in jeans and the girls in micro skirts and midriff tops or short dresses—stood around, some of them swaying to the music thumping through the speakers. Most held red cups of some kind of drink we weren't supposed to have. But we were rich fuckers, and if we wanted vodka and punch or vodka and energy drinks, we got it. Someone always had access.

This wasn't my scene. I didn't like liquor or drugs because both reminded me of my parents' issues. I swallowed hard as I strove to get my emotions back under control. My dad—no, Brad. He was *Brad*, not my relative, and he hated me.

And Aya… She still hadn't responded to my texts. Or maybe she had now—I wasn't sure because I'd turned off my phone after my mom started calling. Pop Syad must have told her about our conversation, but I wasn't ready to deal with her. Not yet.

Maybe not ever.

I needed Aya.

Fuck, I needed to hold her, have her hold me. She was supposed to be at this party. I thought I'd find her here.

Where are you?

My family had been ripped from me—by Brad Porter, by alcoholism, by sex and hedonism, by fame.

Fuck all that. And fuck the assholes who would build their careers on my misfortune. My rage built, fanning higher, and it felt good.

Right. I'd get even. That had always been my way…to get even.

I shoved my hands deep into the pockets of my faded, tattered jeans and stared down at the red Converse on my feet. I probably shouldn't have come here, but staying home in that echoing house was too much. I'd almost asked Steve to take me to Cam's ranch. Mama Grace would have wrapped me in a hug and fed me her peach pie. I loved her peach pie. She would have settled me on the swing afterward and rocked it slowly.

I needed that soothing motion, Mama Grace's soft lilac perfume.

Except I *had* to see Aya.

Lindsay, pressed into a burgundy one-shoulder dress that settled about an inch below her ass and high heels, walked up and leaned against the wall next to me.

"You look unhappy, Nash." She trailed her finger down my chest. I grabbed it.

She smiled, leaning in so those berry-red lips were touching my chin. "Want to make the owie go away?" she murmured.

She was so close, I could see through the makeup to the small, well-covered acne on her jawline.

I pulled back until my head thumped against the wall. "Go away," I snarled.

She thought she was so sly, that I didn't know about the online group where they hated on Aya. But I did. And as soon as I figured out how to prove Lindsay had started it, I was going to take her down.

"Don't be like that," Lindsay said.

I opened my mouth to tell her off, and she slipped something in. Something thin that dissolved as saliva coated it. Reflexively, I swallowed.

"What the fuck was that?" I asked. I turned away from her and spat into the large potted plant nearby.

Lindsay laughed, a truly delighted sound. "Just a little something to get you in the partying mood."

I whirled back and gripped her arms, my rage boiling. "What did you give me?"

Everything quieted, all eyes on me.

Lindsay stood defiantly.

"*What* did you just push into my mouth, Lindsay?" I snarled again, bearing down on her, using my greater height and bulk to tower over her.

She swallowed, thick and hard. "It's…it's…an upper. To…to…make you f-feel good," she stammered.

She didn't look pretty or seductive. She looked cold, calculating…and small.

"I hate you," I said, my voice carrying. "Understand? I. Hate. You. I don't want you near me. I know what you've done to Aya, and I'm never going to forgive you for that. Ever."

Hugh sidled up next to me, grabbing my arm. "Take it down, Nash," he muttered.

"No fucking way. Your bitch of a girlfriend just drugged me."

An array of phones videoed my rage-fueled moment. "You getting this?" I asked them. "She fucking shoved something in my mouth. I don't know what it was—what it'll do to me. And I sure as fuck didn't ask for it."

My head didn't feel right. Nothing felt right. The colors were so bright…and smeared. The music seemed distant. I shook my head. "No. I don't want this," I mumbled. I met Hugh's worried gaze, my wide eyes and pale face reflected there.

"You can't go anywhere," Lindsay said, her tone preening. "You're *high*. You really want people to see you all messed up? Just like your mother." She laughed again.

My mother. My throat convulsed. No one here knew about my parents—yet. But they would. Soon. And they'd look at me just like Lindsay was now. With malicious smiles and whispered words. I hated them all.

"Everyone thinks you're so perfect. The good boy renouncing his parents' lifestyle, but look at you, Nash. No one will think that now." She sneered at me.

I blinked, shocked.

Hate and calculation settled on her face.

"You drugged me," I said again. My words were slurred. I turned back toward Hugh. "She... I don't feel good."

"Oh? Did I?" Lindsay taunted. "Or did you take it all by yourself and now you're too afraid to admit you're as weak as your mommy?"

I shook my head, trying to regain some semblance of normalcy, but everything danced, and psychedelic patterns burst from the edge of my vision in too-bright colors.

I needed Aya. I needed...

As if I'd conjured her, my body vibrated as her perfume drifted to my nose, and in my head, George Harrison crooned his song of love.

Aya. She was here. She could make it better.

I couldn't think...

"I need some water, a...a room."

"I'll be right there with you, honey," Lindsay purred.

I shook my head, and songs burst through my mind. Glorious music. My breath hitched as the notes pelted my brain. "Go away. I need..."

"We'll go get it," Lindsay said, her voice still silky. "I'll make you feel all better." She led me toward the stairs.

"No," I shook my head. "I don't want you. I want water. Steve." He was outside. I'd refused to let him come in, refused to talk to him today. He was giving me space. "Not Aya. Don't want her now..."

Lindsay laughed at that. "You hear him, Stef? He doesn't want Aya."

I paused on the tread. Why was she doing this? She ran her

hands up and down my chest as I stood there, head pulsing, eyes aching.

"All right, honey. You don't have to talk to Aya again if you don't want her."

I turned and there she was. *Aya*. Her eyes were filled with tears, just like my father's. Wait…not my father. *Brad. Asshole*. I shook my head. My mother was an addict.

"I don't want you," I yelled, stumbling away from Lindsay. I wanted Aya.

Somehow, I fell *toward* Lindsay, my face smashing into her ample chest. Her tits were all wrong—too big and they smelled musky. Not like sunshine and some intriguing spice I loved to lick but never could quite place.

"Why, Nash, this is quite the forward way to show your interest," Lindsay said with a laugh.

"Nash," Aya whispered, her voice filled with anguish.

"Go away, you stupid bitch," I shouted into Lindsay's chest.

Lindsay giggled, gripping my head tighter. My hands settled on her hips as I swayed.

For the second time tonight, everything went to silence. The music stopped. I managed to push Lindsay away, and I blinked, searching for Aya. A dull red had crept over her face.

"You heard him, Aya," Lindsay practically sang. "Go away, you stupid bitch."

No. That wasn't what I meant. I struggled upward, out of Lindsay's cushy tits, long enough to catch Aya's gaze.

She lifted her chin before she spun around and pushed through the throng of teens, excited voices following her out.

Snippets of conversation drifted upward.

"*He totally dumped her ass.*"

"*Rejected. So. Hard.*"

Lindsay cackled. "You did what I hadn't been able to."

I started back down the steps, but I collapsed, my head spinning. I needed to get up. Aya couldn't leave. She…she seemed upset. Mad at me.

Fucking Lindsay.

Hugh blocked me. I tried to dodge him but ended up falling. He gripped my shirt, held me close to him so our noses were inches apart. Did he want to kiss me?

"Aya…"

"You're blacking out, man. I called Steve. You need to get help. Stay with me, Nash." He shook me, hard. My head bounced on my neck.

The colors blended in a sick, streaky array. My stomach heaved. Music burst into my head. So much of it—glorious—pushing away the weirdness, pushing away Aya's eyes. My grief and anger. I sighed, closing my eyes, relaxing into the music.

"Oh, leave him alone. He's fine," Lindsay said, her voice sounding far away. "Finally got rid of the stupid goody-two-shoes, thanks to Nash, so now we can cut loose and really part-ay." She finished on a shriek.

"Her mother just died and you drugged him to—what? Try to make Aya jealous? To hurt her feelings? Her mother's dead," Hugh roared.

I flinched. Hugh's voice was too loud. He was pulling me out of the music. If I could just sink back… *Mrs. Didri-Aldringham is dead?* "No," I mumbled. That couldn't be right. I needed to comfort Aya. Why hadn't she told me?

Did I even have my phone? Oh, right… I was avoiding further calls from Pop Syad and my mother.

Hugh shook me, and I slid down the banister, once again seated on my ass.

"Don't feel good," I mumbled.

"You are the worst excuse for a person I've ever met," Hugh yelled. "We're *through*. Get out of my house and don't ever talk to me or to Nash again."

His volume made my head pound, and the music dissipated…whiffs of smoke on the breeze. My head seemed to be trying to split open. I wobbled, the hit finally slamming into my brain and exploding not with ecstasy, like I'd been told, but with more pain.

Aya's eyes. Her beautiful, violet eyes, raised up toward me in defiance and anguish. My dad's eyes—no, Brad's—filled with anger and grief.

I blinked. Steve's face loomed before me, his eyes filled with worry and frustration.

"Drugged," I managed to slur. "Aya… Need her."

Then it all went black.

Chapter 27
Aya

Seeing Nash in Lindsay's arms had brought up every one of my insecurities. She was blond, poised, gorgeous. She loved parties, whereas I liked to stand in the background. She was the exact type of girl everyone expected Nash to go for. Everything *I* wasn't. The Holyoke seniors had invited me to parties begrudgingly, mostly so Nash would come. If he was with Lindsay, one of the glamor girls, there'd be more parties, more chances for those kids to get close to him and his rising fame.

But more than that, I never had fit in. I loved science and worked as a math tutor—superstars didn't date the smart girls. Even Cam, nice as he was, seemed to go for the sleek exterior instead of depth of character. I wouldn't even know how to walk in a short, skin-tight dress.

Those fears, present since before my first day at Holyoke, now choked me. I'd never understood why Nash chose to hang out with me.

Up until yesterday, Nash had never even glanced at Lindsay. And he'd clearly been trashed last night, which was also unusual for him, as far as I knew. I squeezed my hands into fists. Clearly, there were parts of Nash he'd kept hidden.

Just like my mother. She'd omitted that she was *dying*. That's why we'd come back to the United States. Except I never knew.

And I'd never seen how into Lindsay Nash must have been all this time. Why wouldn't he be? She was the girl who made sense for him, the one who wanted to live the rock-star life.

I closed my eyes, but all I could see was Nash with his head in her breasts—his favorite body part—in front of me, in front of our entire class at Hugh's party.

He'd refused to tell me he loved me. For months. Now I knew why. Because he'd wanted to be with Lindsay. My head pounded, and I could scarcely breathe. It was as if I'd forgotten how. Everything I'd once counted on was gone.

I heard pounding on the thick, solid wood front door, and Mrs. Ombly scurried to attend to it. She informed me that it was Hugh, and I met him in the living room.

The room's ceiling soared to dizzying heights, framed in thick bands of crown molding. The walls were covered in damask silk, delicate threads catching the sunshine that peeked through heavy, matching draperies. Seating areas, created with the intent to lessen its vastness, did the opposite because three large area rugs nestled atop the reclaimed wood floors, soaking up the space between the soft, tanned-leather couches and bright yellow accent pillows, each its own distinct cluster.

"Aya, you look bad," Hugh said after he hugged me.

I wore the same clothes I had for days—black leggings and a too-large top that slid off my right shoulder, baring the camisole underneath—the outfit I'd thrown on…what was it? A day ago now? Two? I wasn't sure. I hadn't thought to dress for the party when I went in search of Nash, needing his arms.

My hair shifted, emitting the faint, sharp scent of hospital disinfectant, reminding me of where I'd been and what I'd lost.

I remained impassive, nearly limp in his embrace. "What do you want, Hugh?"

"To be a shoulder for you to cry on. I know you're hurting."

I blinked up at him. "Because Lindsay hurt you, too?"

He grimaced. "About that. There are some things you should know—"

Tears brimmed, and my breath ached in my chest. I whimpered, reliving Nash's harsh, angry words.

Rejected.

Oh, I'd heard them all. He'd promised never to hurt me.

He'd *promised.*

Lindsay's vindictive laugh, her bright, vicious eyes spun through my head.

Whatever Hugh said, I didn't hear, so lost in my own mind.

After a moment, he reached for my arm. "He wants to see you."

I sighed, my hands clasped. "He knows where I am."

Hugh's expression turned befuddled. "Didn't you hear me? He's in the hospital."

I blinked up at him. I'd missed that. In fact, I'd missed everything. "Take me?" I begged.

Hugh nodded, his shoulders relaxing. "There's the Aya I expected."

I gripped the side-door handle the whole way to the hospital—the last place I wanted to be. But I needed to see Nash, make sure he was okay. I couldn't lose him, too.

My stomach flipped. Except I already had.

Something about this entire situation bothered me. I was missing something. Something important.

"Aya?"

I blinked. We were here. I stared up at the hospital building, a sheen of sweat coating my forehead. I didn't want to go in there, didn't know if I could handle hearing Nash was dead. When the doctor had told me about my mother, I'd lost it.

Now, once again, I was supposed to walk in there and have my world fall apart? I shook my head wildly.

"No. I can't. I can't." I slammed my fists against my knees. "I can't."

"Hey. Hey. It's okay," Hugh said. "Look. Cam's there. He would have called if something bad had happened."

I quieted a little. *Right. Yes.* That made sense.

Hugh exited the car and walked around to my side, but I was already out the door, running toward the large glass sliders.

He followed, gasping. "This way." He pointed as we entered.

I froze again. My mind and body numb. *Not the ICU.*

I shook my head, my knees turning to water. I went down hard, shaking.

Hugh had already walked through the doors. I hugged my knees to my chest and rocked. I couldn't go back in there.

"Aya?"

Cam crouched down next to me. I turned in time to catch his grimace, but he stayed on his heels, forearms on his thighs. "You gonna come in and sit with us?"

"I…" I licked my lips. "My mum died." My voice cracked. "Yesterday morning."

Cam cursed. "And now you're back."

"Is he…" My throat closed.

Cam's face contorted. "It's bad."

"How…"

"Drugs. I don't know what."

I whimpered.

"Will…will he…"

Cam sighed. "I don't know yet. Come on. Let's get you inside." He rose with a grunt and offered me his hand.

I wanted to take it. I wanted to go in, but the last time I'd been in there, my mother died. And Nash might, too.

He'd cheated on me, with Lindsay. Humiliated me in front of everyone. Tears filled my eyes.

"I can't."

"All right."

"I…I need to go." I looked around wildly. "I came in with Hugh."

Cam frowned. "I haven't seen him, but I was trying to get the doctor to tell me something. I'll have Chuck drive you."

I must have nodded, and somehow I got to the car with Chuck. As he drove me home, my phone beeped. Dread pooled in my belly, and I whimpered. I wasn't strong enough to look—to see the words. *Nash was dead.* Chuck slid into my driveway and side-eyed me.

"Would you…" I held out my phone.

His big paw touched mine, our fingers brushing. "Need the passcode."

I rattled it off. He opened the app and bit out a low curse.

I snatched the phone from his hand and read the text: *He's mine now.*

I gaped at the photos of Nash wrapped around Lindsay at the party. Below those were a bunch of links to various social media sites. All of them noted that Nash had dumped me because I was too nerdy, too ugly, or no fun.

Chuck laid his hand on my shoulder. "This isn't right."

"This is *exactly* what he chose," I said. My tears dried as I stiffened my spine. "Be sure to tell Cam I'm no longer part of Nash's world. Thanks for the ride."

I exited the vehicle, ignoring Chuck's glower. I headed inside to more notifications. Hundreds of them, all piling on about how I'd never deserved Nash, how I wasn't good enough.

I turned off my phone and sank to the tile floor. Mrs. Ombly found me there sometime later and helped me up to my bed. I huddled there the rest of the night, not sleeping, unseeing, hating Nash Porter for making me love him.

Chapter 28
Nash

Lindsay had doped me up on a breath-mint strip of N-BOMe, which was as potent as methamphetamine and LSD, combined. I was lucky, the doctors said, that she hadn't killed me.

I'd learned that my aggression toward her was a common side effect of the chemicals flowing through me. After such a strong reaction, the doctors had expected me to seize, maybe even go into organ failure. But I hadn't—in part because of the Narcan and sedatives they'd administered to counteract the drug. I'd been pumped with fluids and my vitals monitored all that night and into the next day.

Now, two days after Lindsay's sick prank, I still felt weak and shaky, but mostly I was pissed that Aya wasn't answering my calls.

It was like she'd fallen off a cliff, and I'd been stuck in this bed, unable to search for her. That ended now.

Steve told me my mother was on her way to see me. I stared at him for a long moment, then shook my head.

"I don't want to see her."

"She's worried—"

"Then she should have been around the last couple of years," I snapped.

Steve clenched his jaw .

"I'm serious. I don't want to see her."

"I'll let her know," he muttered before stepping out of the room.

I looked up as Cam and Chuck stepped in, followed by Mama Grace. She scooted around the men and fluffed my pillows, fussing over me. I smiled at her, but my eyes darted back to the door, looking for Aya.

"She's not here," Cam said. He frowned, his brows tugging low over his nose. "She came yesterday, but she fell apart at the ICU doors."

I clenched my fist. "Because of her mom."

Cam nodded, eyes sad. "She told me her mother died."

Mama Grace gasped. "That sweet girl lost her mother?"

I nodded. "Yeah. She's got to be so broken up. They were close. Really close." I clenched my fists, despising my inability to leave, to go to her. "I don't know anything else. I can't get a hold of her."

"About that," Chuck rumbled. "I took her home, and she got a text on the way. It said, 'He's mine now.' And there were pictures of you with some tall blonde."

"Nash!" Mama Grace's hand fluttered to her mouth.

"Lindsay," I croaked. "It had to be. She doesn't like Aya."

My head and muscles ached. All of them. I felt like I'd been beaten with a plumber's wrench.

"She's the one who drugged you," Steve said, stepping out of the corner.

I glared at him, but he held my stare.

"Aya wasn't in a good headspace when she got out of the car," Chuck said.

"Nash doesn't need this stress now," Steve said. "He needs to rest. To heal."

"I need to make sure Aya's okay," I said. "Give me my phone so I can call her."

Steve handed it over, but only because the others watched. His tight expression proved he wanted to deny me.

"Can I get a minute?" I asked.

Mama Grace kissed my forehead. "See you soon, honey."

Cam and Chuck eased Steve from the room.

I dialed Aya's number.

I frowned as the phone rang and rang.

Finally, she answered. "Nash?"

"Ay. Yeah, it's me. How are you?"

"Why are you calling?"

I frowned. Her tone was distant, unlike her normal warmth.

"I wanted to talk to you. To see how you're doing—Ay, I'm so damn sorry about your mom."

"Why?"

I shifted on the bed. "What do you mean *why*? And you don't care that I almost died?"

"I did. I do."

Her tone softened. That sounded like my girl. I leaned back, closed my eyes, and basked in her love.

She cleared her throat. "I saw the pictures and comments of you and Lindsay."

My eyes flashed open. "You have to know that's all bullshit."

"I asked you, Nash. I asked you if you loved me." Her breath broke. "I guess I should have realized, but I still can't believe you did that."

"What are you talking about?" I asked.

"Can't you just stop? You humiliated me in front of everyone," she hissed. "And now—what? You want to be *friends*?"

"I don't want to be friends. You're my girlfriend."

But Aya had hung up. *She hung up on me.* I stared at my phone, my mouth gaping.

I still stared at it when Cam and Chuck reentered the room.

I looked up at them. "She hung up on me. She said I humiliated her."

Chuck's face turned pensive. "The pictures were bad."

"But…"

Cam worked his jaw. "You gotta stay in front of these stories. Now that you're a known name, you're going to get news."

"But Aya didn't believe me."

Cam pulled up a site and pressed play. I watched me, clearly wasted, screaming, "I don't want you."

Lindsay's triumphant smile preceded her arms wrapping around me. She repeated the words to Aya. The camera panned to Aya's devastation. The video cut out.

"It's on YouTube," Chuck said. "It's already got tens of thousands of views."

I licked my dry lips and shook my head. "She has to know I'd never hurt her."

"Does she? Cuz from this angle, that's exactly what it looks like," Cam said.

I met his gaze, feeling desperate. "What do I do?"

He sighed. "Get better. Get a lid on this, best you can. That's what Asher's label's PR team is for."

"But Aya…" I closed my eyes. "I'll have to do those things to get her to listen to reason."

"Pressing charges against the mean girl would go a long way," Chuck added.

When Cam shot him a look, Chuck shrugged. "I hate bullies. You know that."

"I already filed for Nash," Steve said, stepping back into the room. "In fact, there's a detective here who wants to talk to you."

For the next two days, I had to work through lawyers and all sorts of other BS just to get Lindsay charged with the drugging. Luckily, everyone at the party had a phone—and had used it to film me—so the case against Lindsay might just stick. Except that her parents had shipped her back to England as soon as they'd learned about the incident, no doubt hoping to avoid extradition.

But as much as I wanted Lindsay to pay, I was more worried about Aya. She hadn't taken another one of my calls or answered my texts.

And I had to deal with my mother's tear-filled messages, but I held firm, refusing to see her. Steve looked more and more pissed each time he returned to my room, no doubt frustrated with my mother's drama.

Well, that made two of us.

When I couldn't stand it anymore, I called and begged Hugh to go to Aya's house and check on her. I was still stuck in the damn hospital bed, unable to leave, thanks to my heartbeat, which still popped up irregular from time to time. My medical team refused to let me go until my EKG was normal.

"Where do you think you're going?" Steve asked as I ended the call.

I'd risen from the bed, and he hovered nearby. He'd become an autocratic asshole since Brad had spilled my mother's secrets, and I couldn't stand his self-importance, or his supposed—and fake—interest in me.

"To the bathroom," I said. My insides felt like they'd been dipped in acid.

He grunted. "You still not talking to me?"

"Did you manage to talk to Aya?"

"No."

"Are you still the asshole who banged my mom and lied to me about taking a job so you could be near her, not your possible kid?"

He sighed. "Nash—"

"Yeah, we don't have *anything* to talk about."

Steve finally left me to piss in peace. Fuck him. Fuck Pop Syad. Fuck my mother, too.

I pulled Aya's mala beads from the pocket of my sweatpants. I'd taken them the night everything fell apart. I'd planned to give them back to her, but then it all went to shit. I fingered the tassel, wishing it was her soft hair.

Much as I wanted to send her another text, telling her how much I missed her, how sorry I was about her mom, I was afraid. Our conversation yesterday had been frosty—so unlike the warm, sweet woman I'd spent so much time building a life with this past year.

Chapter 29
Aya

The door chimed. My pulse leaped. *Nash.* He would take me in his arms and hold me. This was all a mistake. A terrible mistake. My breath caught, hope surging.

My father strolled into the living room.

"What are you doing here?" I asked. My voice felt dull. I felt dull. Broken. Tired.

"Your housekeeper informed me of Sofia's death."

His jowly countenance neared, and I realized he planned to hug me. I stiffened. "You don't like me."

He sighed as he dropped his tweed-clad arms. "It's never been an issue of like or love, Aya. Life's more complicated than that."

No, it isn't. He'd made it clear he didn't want me around. I wanted Nash to hold me. Except I didn't. My skin prickled with shame. Humiliation flowed over me in a noxious, painful cloud.

My father led me to one of the sofas in the living room. I curled inward once more, not liking the cool, almost clinical feel of the supple leather against my bare shoulder. Everything hurt. Everything. I hadn't known that was possible. My breath hitched, but my eyes remained dry.

"I think it best I take you home," my father announced.

"I don't want to live in England. I'm going to UT in the fall."

My father stood over me, hands clasped behind his back. "We'll ensure you have a spot in a program in England. You'll want family near as you grieve. Perhaps a semester off, to spend time with Harriet and me, would do you good. You can build a relationship with your sisters."

I shook my head. "I don't want to leave. This is my home."

He waved away my words like they meant nothing.

I looked over to see Mrs. Ombly hovered in the open doorway between the kitchen and the living area, clearly unsure how to proceed. I glared at her, angry she'd brought my father into my life. He was already steamrolling my wishes.

"We'll bury Sofia tomorrow," he once again announced, paying no mind to my sputters of indignation. "And we'll fly back for the weekend."

I rose, my hands fisted. "I'm not going to England. *This* is my home."

He raised his eyebrows, which caused his round, fleshy cheeks to jiggle. "Really? And where are all the concerned friends? Your mother's mourners?"

I closed my eyes as he pointed out the truth: no one wanted me. All I'd ever wanted was a home—a place to belong, to be loved. I thought I'd found that here.

I'd been so wrong.

My mother had promised to stay so I didn't end up in this exact position. Nash had promised to protect me. Jeddi had promised to see me cared for.

No one had kept their promise.

Nash should be here.

But Nash had chosen Lindsay. I'd heard his message loud and clear: he didn't want me.

That was the lesson I had to accept. My head swam and my vision blurred a moment. My lip quivered.

Mrs. Ombly wrung her hands as she stepped forward. "Why don't you give Nash a call—"

"We broke up," I said, my voice hard.

For a moment everything was silent. Time stood still, and I felt nothing but emptiness. Maybe…maybe this time moving was smart. I'd start over. Away from Nash. Fuck him if he didn't want me.

"You can get me into a good university in England?" I asked.

My father's smile widened, cutting his pudgy face into two spheres, both lumpy with craters and grooves, much like images of the moon. "With the right sum, one can get most anything, my dear."

I frowned, not liking his attitude. "Okay," I said, settling back on the sofa.

Mrs. Ombly made a sound of distress. "Aya—"

I shook my head. "It's better this way." My voice cracked. "There's nothing left for me here. Not now."

Chapter 30
Nash

It wasn't until Hugh stopped by my hospital room the next afternoon, worry lining his features, that I realized how bad the situation was with Aya.

"She's gone, man," he said as he dropped into the chair next to my bed.

I scowled at Steve, who stood, both sentry and prison guard, in the corner of my room. "I want to talk to Hugh without you here."

Steve's face remained impassive as he took his sweet time strolling from the room. As soon as I could figure out how to get rid of him, I would. Asher would know how to get me new security.

Or maybe I'd keep Steve around and torment him. He deserved it since he'd left me to fend off Brad Porter's verbal abuse for years. Yeah, that's what I'd do. I'd make his life just as miserable as he'd made mine.

I sighed when he was finally out of sight. But I didn't relax. Not with Hugh's comment circling around in my mind.

"Gone? What does that mean?"

Aya and I were supposed to live together this summer. We had the apartment chosen. The lawyers were working to get that awful video taken down. The label had issued a press release explaining that I'd been drugged and there was an ongoing police investigation. Aya had to see all that and realize…

Fuck.

I wanted her to realize *I loved her*—the words I hadn't given her because I couldn't. But those were the only words she'd *needed* to hear.

I flicked at my IV line, restless, miserable. I hated this bed. I hated that I'd been drugged and still felt like shit. I wasn't sure when I'd be able to process what had gone down these past few days. My entire life had imploded. I didn't even know who I was—who my father was.

I looked over, and Hugh was still stalling. "What do you mean, gone?" I rasped out again.

"The housekeeper said her dad came and took her away." His eyes filled with regret, and more than a little guilt. He'd brought Lindsay into our circle. "She's gone."

www.ingramcontent.com/pod-product-compliance
Lightning Source LLC
La Vergne TN
LVHW020043110826
845155LV00029B/625